TREASURES
OF
MORROW

TREASURES
OF
MORROW

H.M. HOOVER

Four Winds Press New York

For Rosie

LIBRARY OF CONGRESS CATALOGING IN PUBLICATION DATA

Hoover, H. M.
   Treasures of Morrow.

   SUMMARY: Two children with telepathic powers,
having spent some time with a more advanced culture,
return to their own primitive society and wonder
where they really belong.
   [1. Science fiction] I. Title.
PZ7.H7705Tr   [Fic]   75-28098
ISBN 0-590-07420-2

Published by Four Winds Press

A Division of Scholastic Magazines, Inc., New York, N.Y.

Copyright© 1976 by H.M. Hoover

All rights reserved

Printed in the United States of America

Library of Congress Catalog Card Number: 75-28098

1 2 3 4 5   80 79 78 77 76

Prologue

On copies of ancient film she had seen the seas turning gray, then brown and thick with scum; seen abrupt and bizarre climatic changes, watched the ugly clouds of smog layering in heavy stillness over the cities, endlessly drizzling dirty rain but failing to clean the atmosphere. As the oceans' enormous masses of plankton slowly died from the filth man continuously spewed into the water, as the oxygen supply generated by the plankton diminished and the air continued to be heavily polluted, as the plants and trees on the land sickened and turned brown or yellow before death, the chain began to break, link by link, and the slow suffocation of life on the earth began.

There was great panic as mankind finally realized the end was near. There was widespread rioting, starvation, disease. Suicide and murder took enormous tolls. But available records covering the decade known as The Death of the Seas indicated that over 93 percent of all living creatures on the earth's surface and under the seas died by simple suffocation.

Fifteen years before that fatal decade, the industrialist Simon Morrow used his vast wealth and power to build LIFESPAN. Into this secret subterranean complex he escaped with his family and a select staff of technocrats. Thus protected, they and their descendants survived the suffocation that choked life from the earth. Six generations later, the

[1]

people of Morrow emerged into an oxygen-thin atmosphere to find themselves alone (or so they believed) for centuries.

But in a remote valley far to the north there were other people, survivors of a military installation, which they called the Base. They, too, believed themselves alone. Where Morrow's history had been carefully and continuously documented, that of the Base had not. The Base retained vague myths of a "Deep Shelter" and fragments of misinformation passed verbally from one generation to the next. They called their leader the Major, their common men "soldiers," and placed great importance on the ability to sire offspring. Solar radiation through the thin atmosphere had made fertility the exception instead of the rule, the "normal" abnormal. Fathers were privileged men of rank.

While both societies were agrarian, the Morrowans, nurtured by LIFESPAN, had retained the knowledge and adapted the usable technologies of the old world. But of greater importance was the fact that, first by chance mutation and then by deliberate effort, they bred a highly intelligent race of telepaths.

Quite by accident, a lone explorer from Morrow chanced upon the Base. He kept his fantastic discovery a secret from his people to conceal the fact that he had violated the Prime Rule by performing an experiment in human genetics. The result of his meddling, as Morrow was to discover twenty-five

years later, was a Base child with Morrowan telepathic sense. It was a sense the child could share with
no one in his surroundings, so he ignored it until it
atrophied. The boy grew up to become the leader,
the Major, of his people. Among his many offspring
were two telepaths: a girl, Tia, and a boy called
Rabbit.

It was Tia who made Morrow aware of the
existence of the Base. From infancy she "broadcast"
her dreams. When she received what she believed to
be "dreams" in return, from Morrow, she was
delighted. It did not occur to her she was unique
until she talked about her dream people and was
punished for lying. Before she grew old enough to
conceal her extra sense, she had been nicknamed
the Witch. And by the time Rabbit was born she was
an outcast. Not until Rabbit was eight did the two
children realize they shared the gift of telepathy. It
was then that Rabbit put both their lives in jeopardy
by accidentally killing a man who threatened Tia.

To save themselves, and telepathically urged on
by Ashira, Morrow's ruler, Tia and Rabbit fled from
the Base. They were pursued by the Major and his
men. After a long and difficult trek, they reached
the coast and the eventual safety of the Morrowans.

This is the story of what happened to Tia and
Rabbit when they left a primitive, repressive society
and entered overnight into a culture centuries more
advanced.

Each day Tia would stand at the ship's rail and look out to sea, waiting. Each day the view was unchanged. To the south and west the waves heaved and swelled, empty. On clear days mountain peaks serrated the eastern horizon. And for all these miles, the land was as empty as the sea.

There came to be a monotony to the view, a sameness, as there was to Tia's thoughts. "We're going home," Ashira had said, and for the rest of them that was true. "But not for me and Rabbit," thought Tia. "We're coming to a place we've never seen. Maybe we won't belong there either."

Almost ever since she could remember, Morrow had been a dream, beautiful, unobtainable. Now it was soon to become reality and if reality spoiled that dream, then she had nothing. And so she watched the horizon and she waited.

During the past two weeks she had become acutely aware of the gulf between her old life and the new. Wearing Morrowan clothes and getting a haircut did not make her one of them. Nor did wishing. She and Rabbit were different, physically and mentally. She was afraid that maybe the Morrowans didn't know how different and when they found out they wouldn't want them anymore. Maybe that was why Ashira said they would have to return to visit the

Base? Tia couldn't think of any other reason why people like the Morrowans would want to go to that place.

Shortly after noon on the seventeenth day the ship rounded the peninsula that sheltered Morrow from the Pacific and entered the outermost reaches of the bay that was her homeport. On a mountainside to the southeast, the mirrors of a solar furnace winked in their geometric march downhill and up again.

As the *Simone II* cruised slowly along, a flurry of small boats skimmed out to meet her, their white wakes and bright sails flashing in the sunlight and sea. To those on board, it looked as if half the population had come out to celebrate the voyagers' safe return. The hulls began to throb with vibration as the ship slowed. For the first time in the quiet of the harbor, the hum of her motors was audible.

Tia and Rabbit stood on the deck where they were trying to see everything at once. For Rabbit the sights were almost all new. He stood open-mouthed with awe, too busy staring to talk or even think. Occasionally, he would reach over, touch Tia, and then point to something. He lacked both words or images to describe his confusion. But to Tia, it was all and more of what she had seen so often in the "dreams." Still even she found it hard to believe she was really here.

Atop the hill beyond the harbor stood Morrow Hall, the winding road to it bordered by tall royal palms. To the northwest, windmills marched along the shoreline like beach toys left behind by an orderly giant. To the east a river wound across the valley and stretched its fingers through marshland to reach the sea. On the gentler slopes above the river, fields made geometric patches and white shell roads led down to the valley where the community that was Morrow lay hidden. Blue mountains edged the eastern horizon, their highest peaks white-capped.

"Tia? Rabbit? Over here!" Looking in the direction of the shout they saw a big catamaran. From its mast flew a long banner that read, "Welcome Home, Tia and Rabbit." People on deck waved up at them and the children waved back.

"That's really n-nice," said Rabbit. "We d-don't even know them and they're glad to see us."

Tia nodded noncommittally.

"Wh-whatever you're worrying about, don't," Rabbit said. "Th-they wouldn't have ba-bothered if they d-didn't like us."

Some of the expedition members of the *Simone II* joined them, eagerly pointing out family and friends in the small boats below, all inviting the children to come visit—or if they wished, to live with them.

"Don't you all live to-together?" asked Rabbit and then looked chagrined. "Was that a dumb question?" he asked Tia telepathically.

"No," she reassured him, "I don't know how they live either. Let's just wait and see."

"Look how p-pretty!" said Rabbit, pointing, and Tia turned to see Ashira and Varas emerge from the doors that led to the main lounge.

Morrow liked its few traditions. Accordingly both leaders were in formal dress for this occasion. Varas wore pale blue. On his wrists were the wide gold bracelets and at his waist the wide gold belt that marked his rank as Elite Emeritus. Ashira wore the white of the reigning Elite, a fabric that iridesced in sunlight so that tiny rainbows flickered as she moved.

As they approached, Tia had a sudden urge to bow, to prostrate herself in awe and gratitude before this regal pair. This emotion-charged thought had hardly entered her mind before Ashira raised her eyeshades and met the girl's look. "No!" came quite forcefully into Tia's mind. "Not now. Not ever."

"How did she know what I was thinking?" marveled Tia as she blushed.

"I have known you since you were two," Ashira reminded her. "You may be able to shut out everyone else, but at this distance there is very little you can hide from me. At least until I teach you how. I should warn you though, there are several other telepaths here with powers similar to ours. But don't worry about it."

"Who else?" Tia wanted to know, and her sense of unease increased.

"Varas, of course. Foran, although he is usually so deeply enthralled by study that he ignores everything else. My second daughter—she is studying at Bonai . . ."

"Will they know everything I think?" asked Tia.

"Not everything, but almost everything you think about them."

"How can I not worry about that?"

Ashira smiled. "Few people object to being thought almost godly—and that seems to be the gist of your impressions to date. Time will give you a more balanced perspective."

All this silent exchange took less time than was needed for the pair to reach the rail where Tia and Rabbit waited. Ashira flipped her eyeshades back down to cut the glare from the water. "We'll be docking in a few minutes," she said. "I know you're both nervous about meeting so many new people at once. So would I be."

"We often argue, Ashira and I, which of us was more frightened during our investment ceremonies," said Varas. "Ashira claims victory because her mind went blank and she had difficulty remembering her name. In my case, they had to delay the ceremony half an hour while I was being sick in the lavatory."

"W-wow!" said Rabbit. "I'm not that s-scared . . . almost though."

The ship was maneuvering along the jetty, the captain letting the swell push them toward the big upright logs that were wrapped in pads to absorb the blow of contact. The faces below came into focus.

Ropes were dropped and wrapped about logs. The anchor rattled down, the deck stopped vibrating. There was a series of hisses and clonks as the loading hatch unsealed and the ramp unfolded to the jetty.

Gold flashed in the sun with a fanfare of trumpets. The crowd fell silent. In the silence the trumpets sang a high clear song. When the anthem ended all stood in shared silence for a moment and then the crew began hurrying down the ramp. Waiting family and friends embraced them. Tia watched the hugs and kisses and wondered at their warmth. No one did this at the Base. Not in public.

Cameras focused on the quartet as they stood waiting at the rail and later when they appeared on the landing ramp. To Tia, who lacked all knowledge of cameras, it looked as if half the people she saw were holding dull metal oblongs in front of their eyes. She supposed the cameras to be another sort of sunshield, like the dark glasses and hoods. Ashira did not attempt to explain the phenomenon of commemorative picture-taking.

"Open your minds," she urged Tia and Rabbit. "You are being welcomed home."

"But wh-what if we get excited and think too loud?" asked Rabbit. "Won't we hurt people?"

She glanced at Varas as if this problem had occurred to them. "We'll take that chance." And when they still hesitated, "Trust me."

Like opening her eyes when she expected to be blinded by light, Tia relaxed her tight self-control by a fraction. It was like hearing gentle smiles. Little by little she let them in until she was smiling in return. "They *are* good," she said aloud, relief and surprise apparent in her voice. "Try it, Rabbit . . . it's like . . ." But she couldn't think of a comparison. "Just try it," she concluded lamely and shared her perception with him. In a moment he let out a big sigh of relief and a grin exposed his teeth to the gums.

As their small procession crossed the jetty, children lining the way gave them flowers until all four were laden with fragrant bouquets. Where the jetty ended and the dock began, a group of distinguished-looking people waited. As Ashira approached, a tall old man stepped forward and bowed deeply. She returned the bow. Tia saw that around his neck he wore the blue and crystal gem she had always seen Ashira wearing.

"I have worn the Gyrestone with honor, madam." The old man said the ritual words aloud, "The Balance of the One is unaltered. No ripple mars our pool of time."

"We who return are grateful, Foran," Ashira responded, kneeling slightly so that he could slip the chain on the gem over her head. "We have been both more and less fortunate." There was a moment of private exchange between them; then taking Tia and Rabbit by the hand she informally introduced them to the Council.

Tia received the impressions of minds operating

on a level she could scarcely grasp. With one exception they too were gentle, kindly if remote, their thoughts distilled to linear simplicity. But that one cold mind—she searched the faces of the Council members, trying to identify its owner. The woman wearing the yellow stone that blazed in the sun? But then the mind retracted and was gone and she couldn't be sure. In all the other minds there was great curiosity, especially where Rabbit was concerned, but no hostility and no contempt toward either of them.

She could almost feel the effort it cost Foran, for example, to remember they had never met. He felt he knew her and it rather surprised him to see her in the flesh, looking up into his eyes. She was not quite what he had expected. "You are only a child, dear Tia," escaped before he reminded himself that, "Yes, I was told that."

Then Foran resumed again in his official capacity. "We welcome you both to Morrow, to your rightful home. This is indeed an historic occasion." Ashira suppressed a smile as he continued. "To gain awareness of your mind, dear Tia, and then Rabbit's, reaching out across time and space, seemed to us a miracle. And now, to welcome you here where you belong gives us pleasure which cannot be expressed in words. May your lives with us be joyous."

Tia and Rabbit bowed as they had seen Ashira bow to him. "Thank you," Tia said in an accent barely understandable to her audience. She could feel the flicker of pleased interest at the sound of her voice, as if they were thinking, "They *are* strangers." And she perceived a new fact, that the sound of one's voice created its own image for the listener, one which might differ from both the physical aspect and the mind of the speaker, and enhance or distract from the transmission of ideas. Unsure of the effect her voice would have if she continued to speak, she simply bowed again. As did Rabbit.

"We have planned a reception for you tonight," Foran spoke informally now, "for you and our voyagers. It will give us all the opportunity to celebrate your homecoming."

While the adults chatted briefly about the trip, Tia and Rabbit shyly exchanged waves and stares with the younger members of the population. A waiting open car was backed onto the dock and the guests of honor led to it.

"One of the Council doesn't like us," she whispered to Rabbit as they got into the car. He nodded, "I know, s-s-specially me."

Morrow Hall was built around a courtyard open to the sky. Within the courtyard was a garden surrounding a lily-starred pool where goldfish gleamed red in the shadows. Paths of crushed shell meandered among flowerbeds and bamboo trees, hibiscus and passion flower vines. In the center of the pool, a fountain rainbowed in the sunlight.

Attracted by the fountain's splashing, Tia and Rabbit jumped down from the car as it pulled up into the shade beneath the courtyard arch and ran to look. As they stood there taking it all in, a small brown dog roused himself from his nap, sniffed the air and gave a "woof!" of curiosity. He stood up, shook himself and trotted over, tail wagging to investigate these new humans.

"L-l-look!" Rabbit blurted, pointing. "Wa-what kind of animal is that?"

"I don't know." Half afraid, Tia stepped back as the dog approached.

"Does it b-bite?"

"Probably not or it wouldn't be here."

"It's b-bigger than a rabbit. Do they eat it?"

"You are seeing your first dog," Varas said as he came up and stooped to pet the friendly animal. "Hello, Bruno. Dogs are pets, animals kept as friends."

[13]

"You don't eat them?" Considering the amount of meat on them, Tia found this hard to believe.

"Never!" The very idea was repellent to Varas.

"L-look at its t-teeth!"

"I can see where your basic orientation will be a bit more—uh—extensive than we had thought," said Varas. "You will see other creatures new to you. Don't be afraid of any of them. It's all right—Bruno is simply getting to know you. Dogs identify by scent. Come, give him a pat."

Tia stretched out her hand gingerly and Bruno sniffed her fingers, then gave her a friendly lick.

"Sometimes they identify by taste, too," said Varas as she made a face and dried her hand by petting Bruno's back.

"What other animals do you have?"

"Cats of various breeds. Cattle, sheep, goats—a truly fascinating animal, the goat. I'm so glad they were a favorite of Simon the Great. Pigs. I've never felt comfortable around pigs. You'll know why when you meet them. Or are you familiar with pigs? I believe they survived in your area. Although I can't communicate with them, they seem too aware, too . . . but it's unfair to inflict my imagination on you. That's right, Rabbit. Rub his ears. Dogs like that. Whereas cats become estatic when properly chucked under the chin."

"What do you do with cats?" asked Tia, ever the pragmatist.

"Admire them. Feed them. They are pets, too."

Varas glanced about looking for a cat to serve as an illustration but there were none in the courtyard. "When you come to my home you'll meet my two favorite cats, Elizabeth and Essex. She's much older than he . . ," and as they missed the allusion, "yes, well. I think we'd better show you Morrow Hall now. Give you a chance to get familiar with the place. You stay here, Bruno. You're not allowed in the house." He led the way from the garden toward the arch where Ashira stood by the car with some other people.

"Morrow Hall is our government house as well as the living quarters of the ruling Elite," he explained as they walked. "A permanent administrative staff lives here and cares for the building, the grounds, and the occupants. Their positions have become almost hereditary. The Hall's Steward, for example, is a direct descendant of the Diaz family who served Simon Morrow in the years before the Death of the Seas. Our chef, Cleone, is descended from the chemical engineers who designed the food supply system for LIFESPAN."

"What's LIFESPAN?" asked Tia but before Varas could reply they had reached the little cluster of people around Ashira. Courtesy required they acknowledge the introductions the Elite was making. In the confusion, Tia forgot her question. There was so much to learn, so many names of people and places and things. They followed the adults across the flagstone terrace.

"Everything s-smells different here," Rabbit observed as he limped along. The foot he had injured during their escape still hurt him. "Not like people live here at all. S-smell."

Tia sniffed obediently, "No woodsmoke."

"No la-latrines. No mud."

"More flowers."

"The grass s-smells greener."

"This building smells like warm stone," Tia was walking next to the stucco wall.

Rabbit put his face against the wall and inhaled deeply. "N-not like s-stone . . ." His face turned red as he saw everyone was watching and listening to them. "M-m-more l-like s-s-sand!" he managed to say.

To Tia's innocent eyes, Morrow Hall once seen became the epitome of architectural beauty. Built originally as a communal house for the first survivors of LIFESPAN, the Hall had been remodeled endlessly over the years. Remnants of other buildings from the world over had been incorporated into it, making it a puzzling but comfortable jumble of styles, vaguely Spanish in overall effect.

Gold had been used rather lavishly in its interior decoration. The metal wore well and resisted the sea wind's tarnish. Gold gleamed from crystal chandeliers and picture frames, door knobs and rail posts.

The main foyer rose the height of the building

and from the entry doors one could walk straight
across the marble floor and out through a matching
pair of doors into the garden. On the right side of
the foyer a wide staircase led to a second floor
balcony which connected the top floor of the south
wing. A chandelier from the ruins of Paris hung
from the high ceiling, its crystals dancing in the light
of tall windows salvaged from Ireland.

Flowers spilled from ancient vases and added
their scent to that of lemon oil and beeswax polish.
From somewhere in the building came the odor of
baking bread.

"And the bread," said Ashira, "what does that
smell of?"

"H-honey," said Rabbit.

"Peace," said Tia, and wished devoutly that that
could be true.

3

In the Great Hall that evening white-clothed tables flanked by red-cushioned benches marched in long rows across the floor. Every flowering plant in the valley had sacrificed the best of its bloom for the centerpieces. Glassware, silver, and plates from a dozen different households supplemented the Morrow Hall supply. Feasts like this were a joint effort. Each household prepared a huge portion of its finest recipe and contributed it to the meal. The Elite's chef and staff made the bread and rolls; the dairy and the winery supplied the beverages.

By the time Tia and Rabbit entered the Hall the tables were set. The chandeliers were lit. On the balcony Varas's string ensemble (minus Varas) provided background music to which few listened. Small children were playing "tent" under the tables and older children ran wild outside on the twilight lawn. Adults gathered in small groups on the room's perimeter or strolled in the courtyard. For all the size of the crowd, there was only a low hum of voices, mostly childish. Mature Morrowans seldom used the slow imprecise verbal method of communication among themselves.

With Varas, the two children stood in an elevated reception alcove just inside the Hall's main entrance. For their welcoming feast, Varas was in

[18]

dark blue; Tia and Rabbit in the simple white pants and high collared jacket all children wore for formal occasions. As newcomers entered, the Steward announced their names for the children's benefit and Varas formally introduced them. They had been receiving for nearly forty-five minutes and the dinner hour was drawing near.

There was a lull in new arrivals and Rabbit leaned on the rail of the alcove and looked out across the room. The tables were crowded with tureens and platters and hot trays. "Boy," he said, "it sh-sure doesn't look like any s-s-supper we've ever seen. Not even on the s-ship. When do we eat?"

"When the Elite arrives and common courtesies have been observed."

"The Elite? Oh, Ashira, you mean. Is s-she like . . ." Rabbit didn't know how to phrase the question politely. "Is s-s-she like the Major? I m-m-mean, do you all listen to her?"

"She is our leader, yes," said Varas, who found odious the comparison of Ashira to Rabbit's late father. "We are governed by our Council of Ten which the reigning Elite heads. The Elite retires at the age of fifty, as I did, and the Council chooses a new ruler."

"Why at fifty?" Tia asked. It seemed very old to her.

"As minds mature they become more static, more self-centered. Total power becomes more and more attractive."

"What if the Elite wants to keep power?"

Varas smiled wryly. "It has happened. A mind became obsessed with rule, unbalanced . . ." He caught her speculative glance. "They are—uh—removed from office for the common good. If you recall the unchallenged power of your Major, total authority destroys all privacy. It leads ultimately to madness. In our society, we are peculiarly vulnerable to the destruction of psychic privacy—particularly since the Elite is always the possessor of both great intelligence and highly focused telepathic powers."

"Can-can they all kill?" asked Rabbit on whom the more subtle psychological observations were lost. His understanding of power was on a much simpler basis.

"The Elites? Yes," said Varas. "But that is not a unique attribute. Or one of intelligence. A good mind, even when unbalanced, does not destroy to retain power. It seduces. But this will come later in your education. Much later."

The gong in the lobby sounded a dull resonant "Bong." Varas ushered them from the alcove and down a short spiral staircase to the main floor. Summoned by the gong, Ashira came in with a group of Council members who were obviously loath to end whatever it was they had been discussing with her. But when she saw the children, she excused herself with a short bow and hurried to join them.

"Does the appearance of the room please you?"

asked a girl who was passing. "It's the first time we ever gave a party this big."

"It's n-nice!" Rabbit told her. "No-nobody *ever* gave a p-p-party for us. Or even a s-s-supper."

"It's very pretty," Tia assured her and, after a hesitant moment, returned the girl's friendly smile.

"Half the town was up here working this afternoon while we napped," said Varas. "I could hear the clunk of tables being set up and linen snapped open."

"We'd better take our places so everyone can sit down." Ashira shooed them down the aisle.

Tia felt awkward sitting at the head table. It was on a slightly raised dais so they could see everyone in the hall and be seen by them. As she waited for the crowd to find their tables she couldn't help but think that if this were her old "home" she would be a servant in the kitchen, waiting for a shout to lug in heavy trays of food and afraid one of the men would deliberately trip her for laughs. Her life and her position in life had changed so radically in the past month that she found it hard to accept. Logic told her she was no longer a pariah. Conditioning was not so quickly changed.

As the last of the people found their places, Ashira rose to speak and silence fell.

"As you all know," she began, "Expedition 81 had its origin almost ten years ago. It was then we received telepathic reception foreign to anything in our experience. At first I suspected that someone was playing an elaborate joke. But after sharing images with Varas and others, we decided they were genuine. They were the dreams of an extraordinary child." She paused a moment, remembering.

"For more than a year, we intermittently saw that mind's fragmented impressions, felt its often painful learning experiences and wondered at their source. We puzzled at its seeming immaturity contrasted to its transmission power. Finally, we (she meant I) succeeded in getting this mysterious transmitter to acknowledge reception of our images. She told us she was three winters old, and her name was Tia. There was no one in Morrow named Tia."

Rabbit nudged Tia with his elbow and grinned at her. She blushed, embarrassed to be the center of attention.

"That we existed did not appear to surprise Tia. That she existed certainly surprised us. We had to accept the startling fact that Morrow was not, had never been, alone in the world. There were other people. But where they were and what they were she could not tell us then. To her we were only part of her dreams.

"Then one dawn the image of a strange cow strayed into my mind through Tia's dream. It was neither my image or Tia's. It was how Morrow first became aware of Rabbit's existence. From that time five long years passed before the *Simone* could set sail to find Morrow's greatest treasure.

"Wordsworth might not forgive me for quoting

him out of context—perhaps the Ancient Literature scholars here will also quiver with indignation. But his words fit my mood tonight.

Here I stand, not only with the sense of present pleasure, but with pleasing thoughts That in this moment there is life and food For future years. And so I dare to hope.

There was a great wave of applause in response to her concluding bow. The ensemble began to play again as she resumed her seat.

"That was ve-very nice!" Rabbit said admiringly. "What happens now?"

Varas took his fork, reached over, stabbed a slice of roast beef and deposited it on the boy's plate. "Now we go to it!" he said. For the next ten minutes the bulk of communication involved the passing and serving of food. The Morrowans were aesthetes but like most aesthetes they were also good trench-ermen.

From the hot trays came roast beef, teriyaki pork, chicken, fillet of giant goldfish, mushroom puffs and—to Tia's delight—onion rings. There were snow peas, bread and rice, tomatoes, crisp salads, corn tiered in golden log piles, fruits and tarts and cheeses, cocomilk and wine, coffee and several teas.

Tia tasted everything and all of it was so good she couldn't decide what she liked best—after the onion rings.

The food on the *Simone II* had been good, but not

of a variety so elaborate or so beautifully served. "I wonder if I'll ever get used to it," she thought remembering the meals of her past where meat was always rabbit or squirrel and not too much of that, and vegetables were potatoes and dandelion greens and nettles in season. At the Base bread was made of coarse cornmeal mixed with acorn flour and baked in corn husks. It was hard and slightly bitter. Only the Fathers were allowed to eat berries or the rare wild honey. She remembered once they had clubbed a little boy for eating honey. She suspected they would kill for a meal like this.

Her plate was dotted with a dab of this, small bits of that. She knew she couldn't fill up on any one thing and still have room to sample what was strange to her. But Rabbit, the purist, took nothing else until he had finished his roast beef. He next chose sweet corn and when only a remarkably clean cob remained, helped himself to a trio of bean pods, then a fish fillet.

"You'll be here eating all night," Tia told him.

"I hope so," was his happy response. "Pass me a mushroom puff."

By the time Tia had worked her way down to dessert, the first of the gift bearers arrived. It was a little girl with a bowl haircut and huge black eyes. She was so short that she had made her way unseen around behind the table and attracted Tia's attention by pulling on her sleeve. When Tia turned, she was startled not to see anyone behind her until she looked down. Wordlessly the little girl held out a small intricately carved wooden box and flashed, "For you," as she thrust it into Tia's hand.

"Why?" Tia had never been given a gift.

The black eyes widened, "To—to put your pretty stones in." Then she thrust a stubby hand into a pocket, pulled out a gold chain and gave it to Rabbit. And before they could say anything, the child ran off.

"I should explain that everything you 'dreamed' about, within good taste of course, is known to all of us," Ashira told them. "We've all taken great interest in your lives. That's how Liane knew about the stones you like to collect, Tia, and of Rabbit's desire for a gold chain like mine."

"But why should they give us things? No one ever did before. And I have nothing to give them . . . what can I give these people?"

An almost palpable veil slipped over Ashira's mind, but not quickly enough to conceal the flicker of pity caused by Tia's distress. "We give gifts because we want to please—or make daily life easier. It is a gesture of caring about one another. There is no ulterior motive behind it, no question of paying or owing. To accept a gift does not indebt you to the giver."

"It's just for nothing?"

Ashira nodded.

It was not the time to educate them on material possessions and relative values, but Tia's reaction to the gift was a warning to Ashira that through ignorance of their adopted culture both Tia and Rabbit could appear rude without ever intending to be. Especially to the children. Tia and Rabbit were chronologically children, but so different from the Morrowan—so crudely cynical and suspicious of others. Watching them on shipboard she had frequently been startled by their reactions and at times she felt sorry for them. Tia expecting to be physically beaten for breaking a plate and feeling grateful when she was not, and then wondering if punishment would be reserved for later. Rabbit nearly drowning in his first bathtub because no one thought to turn off the taps and he was too proud to admit he didn't know how to do something that simple—for fear they'd laugh at him. Tia cringing when anyone touched her, and then wondering why the show of affection—what did the giver want from her? Rabbit, his first day out of bed, denying his leg pained him while he bit his lip at each step—then being disappointed because he wasn't praised for this stupidity.

They were telepaths, quite extraordinarily so, and bright—but still reacting as if dealing with the isolated minds of Simple Talkers. She hated to imagine what sort of people those were who produced fears like these in children. But the fears were there and would remain there until they had time to learn to trust.

She knew she could not erase all their past at once,

and unless she wanted to induce more fear, they must be allowed to associate freely with people their own age. But the children here would have to be advised so their feelings wouldn't be hurt. She would discuss it with Varas later tonight. To Tia and Rabbit she said, "You will both receive many gifts of welcome tonight. Perhaps I shouldn't have kept that as a surprise. But when you are given a gift, simply thank the giver to let them know you find it pleasing."

And so they did as she told them. Mystified but delighted, they were given everything from precious gems to sheepskin rugs, from hiking boots and gloves to paintings. Rabbit, to his great satisfaction, was given a polished disc of agatized wood in shades of beige and brown to wear on his gold chain. By the time the dinner ended, the gifts had mounted until a stack rose behind each of their chairs. Both were worried about thieves. At the Base they would have been unable to keep anything anyone stronger could take from them. Neither had ever had anything they could truly call their own.

"We'll leave it here tonight," Ashira said. "It will be quite safe. In the morning, Manuel can take it all out to Varas's house to put in your rooms."

Even though she was very tired, it took Tia a long time to go to sleep that first night in Morrow. Long after Rabbit had dozed off she lay awake thinking, trying to make herself more comfortable with all the newness. She decided she had liked the party. The food was good, and the gifts—her eyes filled with tears in the darkness thinking how pretty the gifts were. How could she ever pay them back? Not only for the presents, but for everything. How did you tell people how kind you thought they were—without betraying yourself? Without letting them know what you were comparing them with?

The degree of warmth and casualness with which the children of Morrow treated them both pleased and confused her. She decided after some thought that she didn't know how to behave with other children. She had really never known any—other than Rabbit. At home girls had not liked her, the older ones teaching the younger ones to fear her. And the boys there followed the Fathers' example and were scornful of all females of any age. So what little time she had to herself she had spent alone.

Another thing troubled her—those brief flashes of pity she'd felt, not only from Ashira but from other adults. She didn't know what exactly it was.

Pity was not in the ken of the Base. But it carried an assumption of Morrowan tolerance and an assured superiority which she vaguely resented.

For all their intelligence, she thought, there were a lot of things Morrowans didn't know. They had never been hungry or cold. They had never had to live being scared all the time. Even when they were little, nobody ever beat them. And when you *had* to live that way, you had to learn how to put up with it. What right did any Morrowan have to feel sorry for her and Rabbit? The two of them had been smart enough to live through it. She doubted if any Morrowan her age or Rabbit's could do that.

"But they don't have to," her innate sense of fairness reminded her. "There's no way they could, or should, know how to survive as you did. That kind of 'knowing' only makes you scared even when you don't have to be scared anymore. Don't get mad at them for being sorry for you. They don't know any better."

It was very late when the door opened. Tia tensed and then relaxed as she recognized Ashira silhouetted against the light from the hallway. Feigning sleep, she watched her close the door and become a white shadow that moved to stealthily loosen the covers that had twisted over Rabbit's feet, then stand for a moment looking down at her. The fabric of the woman's sleeve whispered as she reached down and lay her hand lightly on Tia's hair. "You'll go to sleep soon," she silently assured her.

Then she tucked up the covers and left as quietly as she had entered. A moment later, Tia heard the door to Ashira's suite click shut.

On the second floor of Morrow Hall, the window of their room overlooked the harbor. Unknown to them, as a precaution against the psychic disturbance they could cause with nightmares or simple dreams, temporary insulation panels had been installed on all surfaces, ceiling, floor, walls, and door. Unlike all the other window screens in the building, an electric cord ran to theirs.

Tia folded her arms behind her head and lay looking out through the screen at the stars winking in the black sky. From the shrubbery below the window, a chorus of insects and tiny frogs sang. She fell asleep trying to identify their voices.

In her dream, Tia was running barefoot across the fields behind the barn. She could hear her mother calling but would not answer. They were all after her, somewhere behind, close to catching her. They wanted to pull her back into the dark. She knew she must warn Rabbit but she couldn't find him. The earth turned into deep sinking sand. She stumbled and began to run on all fours like an animal. And she knew now they would catch her—alone.

The sound of frightened whimpering woke her. Not until she felt the noises aching up from her throat did she know she was making them. She lay still, not daring to open her eyes, not sure where she was, listening to her heart pound in her ears. Slowly the fear-ridden nightmare receded, driven back by the reassuring scents and feel of the bed.

Only then did she become aware of lying on her side so rigidly curled up that her left arm had gone numb beneath her. With a deep sighing breath she stretched out, rolled onto her back, and willed her mind away from the memories. Ashira had said they must go back there "sometime," but not now. Not yet. She was safe here.

An hour later she was wakened again, this time by a dream of Rabbit's wherein his life depended on his ability to speak clearly and he could not, and he was being killed by roars of mocking laughter. She got up, crawled into bed with him and put her arm around him, as much for her comfort as his, and they both went back to sleep.

When she entered her sitting room that night, Ashira was surprised to find Elaine, Council Member and Senior Geneticist, waiting for her. Ashira was not pleased. It had been a long day, the climax of a long trip. She was tired, she wanted some time alone, and she was not overly fond of her visitor to begin with.

"I must speak with you," Elaine began with her usual intentness. Elaine always gave one the impression that her interests were not only far more important than anyone else's, but that the other's interests were nonexistent. "I have been studying the two refugees since they arrived . . ."

"Why are you speaking? Your voice might wake the children."

"It's because of them I am speaking. I don't want them to know. You don't really know the extent of their reception. Coupled with their violent primitive origins . . ."

"Don't be paranoid." Ashira was irritated. "Besides their room is shielded in case they dream."

"Well, at least you thought of that."

"Just what is it that can't wait until tomorrow?" The Elite's tone was cold.

"The lack of specimens! I understand you had to

shoot some of those creatures. But you brought back nothing but these two children. No tissue, no blood, bone—nothing. What did you do with the bodies?"

"We buried them."

"You what?"

"You heard me."

"Was there no room in the ship's freezers?"

In spite of herself Ashira got the picture Elaine had in mind—the body of a Base man hung like a carcass of meat. She blocked it out, but the impression lingered. "I find your lack of sensitivity monstrous," she said bluntly.

"And I find your lack of clinical detachment beneath your rank," snapped Elaine. "To waste a chance like that to further anatomic and genetic research in human environmental adaptation! For all you know, you have deliberately imported genetic disaster. I must have the opportunity to study these two specimens. I will try to be as fast but as thorough as possible. I would estimate that my requirements will take me no more than thirty days. With the help of my staff, of course. We will work in LIFESPAN. If you will explain my needs to the specimens, make them willing to cooperate, I would appreciate it . . ."

Elaine's rapid speech sputtered to a halt as she was finally forced to acknowledge the anger she had evoked. Elaine had never before felt threatened by an Elite, but she did now and her face paled with shock. It had apparently not occurred to her that her demand was either offensive or would be refused. It had been more than two hundred years since an Elite had telepathically executed a Morrowan in anger. Now Ashira let her visitor know exactly how close that record was to being broken. She held the threat until its full implications had been absorbed by Elaine's egocentric mind.

"Since you seem to prefer it, I'll return to verbal communication," Ashira said. "May I remind you that it was a geneticist who created this particular problem thirty-five years ago? And that the decision to bring the children here was not simply my personal whim. And that you raised no objections to their coming."

"Granted. But regardless of the origin, we may have a potential problem. Don't allow compassion or idealism to subvert our interests."

"Morrow's interests—or yours, Elaine? Look, I know what a temptation it must be for you to have two unique living 'specimens' practically under your nose—don't interrupt. You will listen to me and you will understand. Inform your staff that you *all* are to leave Tia and Rabbit alone. If I find you have in any way added to their trauma of adopting to this culture, you will be tried by the Council of Ten. Should that happen, I would issue an Edict of Total Exile. Good night."

She rose and opened the door.

"I shall put my request before the Council in the morning," was Elaine's parting shot as she left. "We'll see who's barbarous."

"I'm sure you will." Ashira stood in the doorway to watch the thin little woman go down the hall and then listened to her footsteps descend the stairs and echo across the lobby. When the heavy entry door closed she gave a sigh of relief. Then on impulse, she went down the hall to check on the children again. This time Tia was asleep too.

Before she went to bed, Ashira called Thomas the Night Steward on the intercom. "Keep an eye on the children's room," she said. "I don't want them disturbed by anyone."

In the morning Elaine kept her promise and made her request to the Council. They considered it in silence, human computers engaged in data retrieval and analyses.

"Pointless," Lora Sandis, Senior Medical Officer decided. "All tests were run when Tia and Rabbit boarded the ship. Their skins are tougher and darker than ours; their lung capacity greater—the former due to solar radiation exposure, the latter to higher altitude. All results are available if you want them. Nothing genetically unique showed up."

"You are not the ultimate authority in genetics," Elaine's response implied her own authority.

"Perhaps I missed something, Dr. Balchan." Foran was, as always, very formal. "Why isolate the children? All that would indicate is their reaction to the stress of unjust imprisonment. Nothing applicable to their life here."

"But it is—or could be!" Elaine insisted.   "Both

have extraordinary telepathic ability. We know the male has lethal concentration powers. Does she? Do we know their mental stability—what they are capable of doing under stress? If they are frightened, would they kill whomever threatens them?"

"In which case you would be the first to go," purred Lora.

Ashira interrupted. "We have known both minds for years, both at conscious and unconscious levels. I would trust Tia and Rabbit in any situation they might encounter here. I am thoroughly opposed to Elaine's request and revolted by the thinking which prompts it."

"Do I sense the irrationality of prejudice where these children are concerned?" Lora Sandis wondered. "Or the irrationality of passion for pure research?"

"You sense the discipline of a scientific mind," Elaine answered. "Something you seem to lack. Because they appear harmless you would jeopardize us all. What are they really like? What will their offspring be? We don't know. With a little cooperation I could tell you precisely the telepathic and genetic strengths of both, project their potential development . . ."

"To what end?" asked Varas. "Because we are capable of a thing is no excuse for doing it. We know as much about Tia and Rabbit as anyone has a right to know. We would not violate the civil or psychic rights of any citizen born here. I will not vote to permit you to violate theirs."

"If I were Elite it would be done!" Elaine assured them darkly.

"It is because of your tendency to the extreme that you do not hold that office, Madam," Foran replied, "in spite of your ability."

The vote was unanimously against her.

Tia woke up to a whistler warbling a song of infinite variations and subtle shadings of half tones. There was a moment of shock when she opened her eyes and saw the strange room, then remembered where she was. She lay listening, marveling at the whistler's skill—until it occurred to her that the tones were not human. Careful not to disturb Rabbit, she slid out of bed and went to the window.

A herd of short-legged white woolly animals was feeding on the grass halfway down the hill. Occasionally one would raise a black muzzle and ask "Maaa-a?" but so far as she could tell, none was musically inclined. A flash of yellow across the shrubs caught her eye, then a second and a third flash as a flock of canaries dipped to light on the bushes. The branches barely trembled. "Rabbit! Wake up! They have flying flowers!" At her excited cry the canaries flew away. She was very disappointed. The whistling stopped, too.

A new sound caught her attention, a soft squeaking and then a thump as a boy on a bicycle came coasting around the corner of the Hall and across the bumpy lawn. His hood was off and when she saw his face, Tia gave an involuntary "Ah!" of surprise. His resemblance to Ashira was startling. It was like seeing her as she must have looked as a child.

The boy braked to a stop and posed with his left foot on the pedal, right leg stretched to keep his balance, and looked up at their window. Seeing her, he smiled. "Mother thought you'd sleep late, but I didn't think so. I'm Simon, Ashira's son. I get to show you around today. Where's Rabbit?"

"He's still sleeping . . ."

"I'm n-not!" Rabbit protested from his bed. "Who is it?"

"Simon. Ashira's son. Come look!"

"I didn't know s-she had any ch-children." Rabbit kicked the sheets off, slid off the bed and hurriedly limped over to join her. "You never s-said she had ch-children. Hi, Simon . . ." Then, seeing the bicycle, "What are you s-sitting on?"

"Get dressed and come down. I'll show you. I'll wait for you in the dining room." With a push, Simon coasted in a circle and pedaled off toward the front door.

"I g-get the bathroom f-first!" and Rabbit dashed off, grabbing his clothes as he went. "Does Ashira have any other ch-children you didn't tell me about?" he called through the bathroom door as Tia was dressing.

"Two. Celene is fourteen and she's studying at Bonai—that's where Morrow's new settlement is— and Elizabeth is sixteen and she is away. She's studying something but I didn't understand what it was. Something about the stars."

"Who are their F-fathers?"

Tia shrugged. "I don't know. Hurry up in there. It's your turn to make the beds."

Simon met them at the foot of the stairs and greeted first Tia and then Rabbit with a hug and a kiss on both cheeks. Tia found it startling, but pleasant. Rabbit looked wide-eyed up at Simon. "How come you d-did that?" he demanded, half indignant.

"We always kiss people we're glad to see. Don't you like being touched?"

"If people m-mean it nicely," Rabbit said thoughtfully. "I n-never thought about it before, but I guess I do. I like it when Tia touches me—and Varas and Ashira. And Dr. Lora's hands make you f-feel good. But where we come from, the only time we got t-touched was when s-somebody hit us."

Simon frowned, but good manners kept him from asking questions. "I'm glad you're here with us," he said.

"Me, too," said Rabbit, eager to change the subject. "Let's g-go eat."

Simon led the way. "I wanted to meet you yesterday but my teacher said I had to stay with Clara until she had her baby. Clara is my cow. I have three cows now. This is Clara's second calf. I didn't give him a name. We have enough bulls so we raise male calves for meat and I don't want to get to know him personally if we have to eat him. Did you have any cows?"

"Not our own," said Tia.

"B-but there were cows," said Rabbit. "I liked them. Can we see yours?"

"Sure, but they're nothing special. There's lots more important things to see."

That reminded Tia, "I saw flying flowers this morning. Right before you came. And someone was whistling."

Simon stared at her, puzzled. "Show me." She flashed him an image and he stifled a smile. "Those were canaries," he told her. "Birds."

"B-birds? Aren't th-they all dead?"

"The wild ones are. But our birds all come from Morrow stock." He counted them off on his fingers, "Chickens, geese, ducks, turkeys, parrots, para-keets, canaries and—uh—finches."

In the dining room Cleone, Morrow Hall's chef, served them.

"Wh-what's for breakfast?" Rabbit asked.

"How hungry are you?" she wanted to know.

"Starving."

"Well, in that case, two bran muffins, six sausages, chopped fruit with coconut and a mug of warm cocomilk."

"N-no coffee?"

"No coffee."

"Even with lots of milk?"

"No coffee. Tia, what would you like?"

"Eggs and fruit and a muffin."

As they ate, Simon tried to satisfy their curiosity about birds. "The canaries and finches were allowed to go wild again. But the parakeets and parrots eat too much fruit and grain. And they raise families awfully fast. So they are house pets. We turned some loose far from here—on another continent—just to see if they'd make it, but nobody's dared to do it here. They might upset the Balance. There are no predators to keep their population in control. Like the cats and dogs could go wild—and eat up all the small animals—and then starve to death. So we don't dare release them. I see I've confused you. Don't worry—you'll understand soon."

"I hope so," Tia said, but doubted it. There was so much to learn. "I'll have to study all my life."

"Everyone does," Simon grinned and stood up. "Let's wash up our dishes and go. We're taking mother's little car because of Rabbit's foot."

It was difficult for them to decide what they liked most among all the things Simon showed them that morning, besides the fact that everyone seemed glad to see them. Tia liked the machine shops and all the myriad equipment while Rabbit could barely be dragged from the garages. The solar furnace was the most spectacular, but still beyond their comprehension, as were many of the things they saw. (They had difficulty believing light bulbs were not magical.)

The farmland pleased them and they could appreciate the animals, the cows, pigs, sheep, goats, and even the domestic fowl. The fields were deep-loamed and rich and familiar as nothing else. And the pony tractor units appealed to Tia. She had spent days planting by hand what these machines accomplished in minutes.

Everywhere they went people were working. From children of six to the oldest adult they worked in the barns and fields, on the roads, in orchards and greenhouses. Like the delicate plants, the younger children were kept inside the shaded areas. If it could be avoided, no Morrowan felt the direct radiation of sunlight upon his face for more than a few minutes at a time.

Ancient man had polluted and depleted earth's atmosphere and the ozone layer of its stratosphere; the shielding once afforded against infrared and ultraviolet radiation was diminished. Now relatively short exposure produced burns, retinal damage, and bizarre cell growth.

The houses of Morrow made a great impression on them. No log houses these, but brick or stucco, tile and glass. Some families, like the Wus and the Sandis, had large sprawling complexes wherein the several generations lived. Not everyone lived in the town. Many, like Varas, had built in the foothills beyond. All people, Simon told them, regardless of age or position, had at least a room of their own and an inalienable right to privacy. This, to Tia and Rabbit, was the peak of luxury.

"At Varas's house, will *we* each have a room of our own?" she asked Simon in wonder.

He nodded and swerved the silent little car around a cat sleeping on the warm path.

"Does anyone else live with Varas?"

"Not now." For a moment, it seemed as if Simon would explain but when he did not, Tia's curiosity was aroused. She'd never really thought about other people in Varas's life, and there must be some. But he never mentioned any. And that reminded her of Ashira.

"Where is your Father, Simon?"

"He—uh—he died." Simon said the last two words very precisely as if to set them apart and separate from himself. But he couldn't control the sense of loss that flooded his mind and Tia and Rabbit both realized with a shock that this boy had loved his father. Which was very strange to them. No one loved any father at the Base—even if they knew which one was theirs.

"There's the central granary." Simon obviously wanted to change the subject and Tia was too shy to ask any more questions. But when she saw Ashira and Varas at lunch she looked at them with new interest.

From noon until after 3:00 all work stopped in Morrow. The sun was directly overhead, hot and dangerous, a good time for a siesta. When the luncheon dishes were washed and the last clink of glassware and silver stopped, everyone took a nap.

In the human hush the faint hiss of the surf became noticeable again; an occasional cow would bawl and another answer from a dome across the valley; a hen sang out from a hidden nest in the bushes and then fell silent as if suddenly self-conscious.

Unaccustomed to this lull in her days, Tia lay wide-eyed on her bed, waiting, listening, impatient to get on with things. She wanted to get to Varas's house, to see her own room and it seemed forever until she heard Simon's running footsteps in the hall outside and heard him call, "Hey, you two. Are you going to sleep all afternoon? Everybody's ready to go—except Mother."

They followed Simon down to find Varas waiting in the driver's seat of a flatbed truck. And on the flatbed was an assortment of children, Bruno and another dog, and several wardrobe cases. Tia recognized Liane.

"This is Hajime, that's Max, Bobby . . ." Simon introduced them all. "We all decided to go along with you and see how you liked the place. Climb up!"

Where Morrow Hall by its very size impressed but intimidated, Varas's house comforted. With its red tile roof it clung like a rusty limpet to the rocks on which it was built. There was no lawn but well-placed pines scented its air, and wildflowers bloomed amid stone and pine needles more artfully than nature would have bothered with. Beyond the orchard tree tops, the entire valley spread out below the lanai. Varas had chosen the site both for its panoramic view and because it was well back from the sea.

The spacious kitchen was equipped to handle any variety of jobs, from preparing dinner to repotting shrubs. Varas had made what would have normally been the living room into a rehearsal studio whose deep windows overlooked the sea winking in the distance. The walls were lined with bookcases full of scores and files for sheet music. A concert grand dominated one corner of the room; the opposite wall was an instrument closet. On one windowsill two fat tiger cats regarded the newcomers with vague interest, and then returned to contemplating the view.

"Meet Elizabeth and Essex," Varas said by way of introduction, but noticed Tia and Rabbit were no more interested in the cats at that moment than the cats were in them. What they wanted to see was their own rooms. "We go down this hall," he said, and led the way, "to Tia's door."

"Wh-where's mine?"

"Close by. Tia . . ." Varas stretched out an arm to hold the other children back.

Like a cat entering a strange room Tia stood in the doorway and looked the place over. It was large, and rich with colors of beige and brown and russet. The tile floors were softened by fleece rugs. In the lounge area were easy chairs, a big worktable with empty shelves above it, a well-stocked bookcase, and sofa. Beyond in a raised, windowed alcove was her bed and doors leading to her dressing room and bath.

When she entered, it was to slowly circle her space, touching each item of furniture, the drawer pulls, the fabrics; feeling, getting to know the place. She could not really accept the idea that all this was hers, that people would give her so much. Her chin quivered and she bit her lip to conceal its betrayal.

"We will leave you to put away your gifts from last evening," Ashira suggested tactfully and pointed to the neat stack in a corner. "While Varas gets Rabbit settled, the rest of us can go out to the kitchen and get some cold drinks ready. We must have something to toast the occasion."

Those initial weeks at Varas's home were the first peaceful, pleasant time in the children's lives, as they were deliberately designed to be. They were simple days, their routine definite but not compulsive. In the mornings, they worked with Varas in the orchards. The hours immediately after siesta were given over to study with Varas as their tutor.

The peaches were ripe when they arrived. And they learned their teacher's passion for peaches as he allowed them to help pick the first small crop of his "Blushing White" tree, an honor allowed no one else. It was, he told them proudly, the first white peach ever grown at that altitude and longitude and he felt it his finest contribution to advanced civilization.

For Varas, fruit was as much a matter of aesthetics as nourishment. He could spend minutes admiring a perfect fruit—the way a leaf had left its shape outlined across a cheek, a skin like old ivory or yellow with just a hint of jade. He would weigh their roundness in his hands, inhale their fragrance. He could break open a ripe peach without bruising its flesh and expose the frosty red oval where the seed nestled. Sometimes as Tia watched him she got the distinct impression he was praying.

It was all part of their education, this work. He showed them how he cut and taped a graft so that new life flowed into it from the parent shoot. "We are grafts, Rabbit and I," thought Tia. "I wonder if we will 'take'?" They learned to shade and weed and hoe the vegetables that grew between the tree rows. And they could spend hours lost in their own thoughts if they wished, or talking to the people who worked with them. For this was an ideal way to become acquainted, with the task at hand as a common meeting ground.

Tia found to her great surprise that she, who had always felt a weakling, could work harder and with less effort than most Morrowans. And her pride in that knowledge gave her new confidence. Perhaps she wasn't worthless after all.

Another thing surprised her—the failure of most of the Morrowans to realize how well off they were. "You are so lucky!" she told Simon one morning as a group of them picked peaches together. "You have all this wonderful food, warm or cool clothing, good houses and tools, and kind people . . ."

"Roofs don't leak and nothing stinks," added Rabbit.

"That's not lucky," said Simon's friend Max. "We've always had that."

"We didn't," said Tia. "And you can study and learn everything about anything . . ."

"And when you've learned it," said Simon, "who do you tell it to?"

"What do you mean?" Tia was puzzled.

"I mean, we're smarter than any of the old civilizations. But there's no one else to care what we are—or do. For example, my sister, Elizabeth, says the neutron star in the Crab Nebula is winking out. Once that news would have excited astronomers all over the world. Now it excited about six people. Even Mother didn't really care."

"I see stars winking," little Liane said. "They wink all the time."

Tia tended to agree with her; she didn't understand what Simon was saying. Who cared if a distant star winked out as long as everything else was safe? "I don't know," she said, "I can't think of a better way to live than this."

"You s-should see our . . . where we l-lived before," Rabbit said.

"Elizabeth says Morrow is a velvet box and we're all shut inside and no one will ever open the lid." Simon flashed Tia the concept and she considered it for a time.

"Then we'll have to push it open ourselves, that's all," she said. "Besides, that's just an imaginary thing. We're real."

Rabbit had never done field work before. At the Base that was left to women. At first, because of his foot, he got to sit and sort peaches. Those spotted with brown-rot had to be hurried down to the packing houses to be made into jam. Of the prime fruit, those not for immediate table use had to be peeled and frozen or canned. To Rabbit's great delight Varas taught them both to drive the little trucks and when a load of crates was ready, Rabbit usually got to haul it down to town.

From the top of a ladder where she sat picking, Tia watched him drive off down the hill road one morning. He was wearing a broadbrimmed straw hat and eyeshades hid half his face but the pride in him and the grin on his face as he bumped the truck along kept her smiling for the next hour.

She was beginning to find life good. She loved learning new things, and being busy kept her from worrying. Once Varas had assessed their basic fund of knowledge, most of which he himself had communicated to them over the years, the first skill he taught them was writing—with a pen instead of a stick on sand. Then he taught them how to bake bread. The lesson included everything from taking grain from the granary to the mill to be ground, to yeast, to the moisture-retaining qualities of honey over sugar. The bread lesson took two weeks and when they were through, they could not only make a tasty batch of bread but knew how to use the stove and warming oven, go to the village warehouses and the mill, identify wheat, rye, and oats both growing in the fields and milled, recite what by-products the straws produced through fermentation and at what temperature yeast died.

Varas wrote down a list of books and tapes available on all phases of the subject should they wish to know more about it, and then he introduced them to the building buried in the earth which Morrow called LIFESPAN.

8

A quarter of a mile square and forty floors deep, equipped with vastly intricate regenerative life-support systems, LIFESPAN remained a functioning tribute to the technological genius of the Last Century of the old world. Built by the industrialist Simon Asher Morrow, LIFESPAN enabled him and the technocrats he selected to not only survive the disaster, but their descendants to endure until the earth's fragile atmosphere would once again support human life.

For Rabbit, LIFESPAN was a place of wonder, each of its seemingly endless floors more fascinating than the next. He liked to hear over and over again the story of its history and that of the people it had sheltered and marvel that all this had happened before he was born. But he was also glad that "nobody has to live locked inside any more."

For Tia the great building, and in particular its library and screening rooms, became an Aladdin's cave, a source of treasure in the form of knowledge.

"In these rooms and the auxiliary banks below is stored almost all that Morrow knows," Varas had said as they entered the library. "If you wished to, you could stay here all your life and still not begin to learn a tenth of what is available."

"Is that true?" Tia asked, feeling beaten before she started.

"Literally? Probably not," he admitted. "There's no reason for anyone to commit too much to memory. It's all here for referral. Much of the technical literature is obsolete or impossible for us to utilize. Even Simon Morrow did not anticipate the true finality of The Death of the Seas. He had counted on survivors—other than his descendants."

"He was right," said Tia. "We—the Base survived."

"Yes, but not in quite the manner he envisioned survival . . . a technologically advanced society . . ."

"But could *I* study here?"

Her eagerness pleased Varas.

"Of course. All that is Morrow is yours."

From that time on she came there almost daily. At first, like a child tempted by too great a choice of toys, she sampled this and that, staying with nothing long. The computer played music for her, read poetry, ran old videotapes, recited genealogies of generations past.

But she found herself unable to absorb so catholic a diet. It was too much information, too foreign to her, and too fast. And so she turned to books. These she could take at her own pace, hurrying through them, or pausing to puzzle or daydream as long as she wished. And she wished.

Rabbit came with her sometimes, but what was a passion for Tia was a pastime for him. He liked to learn about what interested him but he had no urge to know things just for the sake of knowledge. And sometimes going sailing or bike riding or just play-

ing with the other children had more allure than the
idea of taking the elevator down to the quiet of
LIFESPAN's thirty-seventh floor. More and more,
but now by choice, Tia again spent many hours
alone.

Ashira, who understood Tia better than Varas
did, did not approve. She knew Tia had never had
time to play, had never learned how, and she
suspected that part of the girl's passion for books
was prompted by her unease with people her own
age. To Ashira it was more important that Tia first
become whole than learned. And so one evening
when Varas let Tia stay late with them, rummaging
in the library while he and Ashira researched a project, Ashira decided it was time to discuss the situation.

"If we are not careful, we are going to create a
learned hermit. Tia is trying to absorb everything in
the library."

"She wants to please us," Varas closed his book but
kept a finger in it. "She's afraid of disappointing
us . . ."

"And to avoid disappointing she risks alienating?"

"She prefers solitude, I think," thought Varas.
"There is no danger of Rabbit retreating to an ivory
tower. Not because he lacks the intelligence, but his
disposition is not that of a solitary. He had enough
approval if not love, to halt the warp of his development."

"Tia is not warped. She's . . . inhibited," admitted

Ashira. "She's been forced to hide within herself to survive. But she's beginning to relax with us, slowly, thanks to you—but I don't think we should encourage her to hide in study. Besides, some of those ancient books could cause her psychic indigestion. She still can't discriminate and she swallows everything whole."

"She is the perfect audience." Varas seemed saddened by the fact. "You know, I see us through her eyes sometimes—each one of us, young and old, more than eager to have a new listener to our pet passions and peeves. Each assuming she will be impressed as well as educated. Because she knows it gives the speaker pleasure and she wants to please, she takes it all in, the information as well as the ego. And at times she finds us a bit naïve. When she comes here to the library, I suspect she's taking refuge as much as seeking knowledge. Listening is very tiring."

"I don't think she listens merely to be gracious," guessed Ashira. "She's waiting for us to betray ourselves."

"Who?"

"You—me, all of us. She covers it well, but I think she's afraid that one day, perhaps, one of us is going to say or think something that makes everything she wants to believe about Morrow a lie. And she doesn't want to be too disappointed."

"That poor child," Varas's sympathy went beyond mere pity.

"Somehow, we'll have to get past that wall of suspicious reserve. I'm not sure how. How do you establish trust in a mind that has known too much betrayal?" She took a deep breath; the subject was depressing her. "I want them both, but especially Tia, to be more secure by the time we go to the Base this spring. She dreads going so. If you agree, I'm going to begin training them in controlled telepathy. It's time they learned mind-sharing."

He thought it over. "I think they're ready, yes. You'll be taking them to the Retreat for training?"

"No. If they could receive and transmit 3,000 miles, going twenty miles out to sea wouldn't help much. The best training place is here in LIFESPAN. That way if there are any problems, it will be confined to one room or floor."

"Are you afraid?"

"Of Rabbit? A little. He gets quite . . . exuberant."

"I could do it, you know. I'd rather, than risk you. Life has been good to me."

"No. I won't permit that, Varas. For completely selfish reasons. Any more than I would permit either child to harm me, even accidentally."

The telepathic training period with Ashira made anything else Tia and Rabbit would ever learn seem simple by comparison. It was not that Ashira was stern; she simply expected everyone to do their best. She would not accept less.

"There is no excuse in Morrow for misunderstanding," Ashira told them when they began. "You are capable of projecting clarity and detail. And receiving in similar style. You shut us out now all too often because of fears you will not share. We cannot allay these fears until we know what they are. Nor can we intrude; not I, nor anyone else. But, so long as you retreat into your minds, it's as if you carried your shielded room with you—like a snail with its shell always on its back. I will teach you to truly communicate—so that you may learn to trust, so that the past which made shielding necessary will lose its hold on you."

Tia was sure that speech was meant more for her benefit than Rabbit's. She was right.

Training half-grown telepaths to use that sense was as new to Ashira as learning was to her pupils, so she began with simple things and kept the training on an impersonal level. She wanted them to experience perception and awareness, not added self-consciousness of their differences.

Rabbit's first discovery, for example, was that on a simple thought like wanting a drink of cocomilk, it was not just the word "cocomilk" he transmitted but also flavor, scent, and the cool smooth texture in his mouth. Mixed up with that was a blurred image of ivory milk in a red glass, white teeth (his), anticipation of enjoyment in drinking it, and a dozen other associations with meaning only to him. To flood a disinterested bystander's mind with this wealth of trivial sensory detail was not only unfair, but the ultimate Morrowan insult—boring.

So Lesson One was learning to discriminate, to edit out the obvious. The ability to edit led to control. They practiced transmission and reception first of flat, one-dimensional images with literal meanings; then concepts with focus, shading, definition, and perception; emotions by degree, depth, and association.

As speech lost its great importance, gradually and without any conscious effort, Rabbit's stutter disappeared. As if, now that he no longer had to talk, he felt free to do so.

After three months they could learn outside of LIFESPAN and the shielding on their rooms was removed for they had conquered their lifelong habit of transmitting in their sleep. It was the ability to control that Tia appreciated most. When she had absorbed enough to stop transmitting her dreams she began to relax. Now at least her subconscious mind would no longer betray her.

Later in their studies they would find parallels to this basic telepathic training in music composition and theory, in physics, and in the workings of the scanning electron microscope. Gradually, they began to appreciate the almost limitless potential of this sense. And to understand that Morrowans used speech as much as they did to retain an identity apart from the "commonsense" of the community.

As her pupils grew more adept, Ashira slowly began to incorporate some basic education into their study. Multiplication tables and metric system were easily visualized, sheet music lost its mystery as each flagged dot on the barred sheets was seen to be a note. And in turn she had them teach her to speak the language of their former home.

Tia was not sure why Ashira would want to learn that. She had been hoping as the months passed that Ashira would forget about wanting to go back there. Ashira had said the two of them would go back as guides and interpreters. But if she spoke the language, why would she need them? Maybe they wouldn't have to go along. When telepathy training began, spring had seemed a long time off and Tia could hope that Ashira would change her mind. But spring and Ashira kept constant. Tia kept telling her that there was nothing at the Base that could possibly interest the people of Morrow. Ashira thought otherwise.

Now Expedition 82 was in the final stages of preparation. The thought of going back could be ignored no longer. It haunted all of Tia's waking hours. Just the idea of seeing her old home again gave her stomach pains.

"If I got sick, I couldn't go," she told Rabbit one night when they were discussing it. Varas's quintet was rehearsing in the music room and the two, along with the cats, had fled to the lanai outside to watch the stars come out.

"Ashira might just wait until you were well again."

"I know," Tia admitted, and petted Essex as he wound himself about her ankles.

"Maybe it won't be so bad. The Major's dead—he can't hurt us again. Besides, I'd like them to see us." He grinned to himself, pleased at some private daydream. "Can't you see their faces when they see us again? Boy, are they going to be surprised! I bet they think we're dead in the woods someplace."

"Either that or they'll still want to kill me."

"But they can't. Not now. Ashira and Varas and everybody won't let them. And wait until they see the amphibians!"

"They'll just yell and run like the hunters did that night."

"I didn't get to see that." It was one of the big disappointments in his life.

"You'd have liked it. They were really scared! They ran . . ."

"What happened to them then?"

Tia's brow furrowed. "I don't know. The Major tried to stone you and Ashira shot him. But the rest . . . nobody ever said."

"They're probably dead," he said matter of factly.

"I don't care. I don't want to ever see any of them again. Or that place."

"We won't be there long. I asked Varas. He said a week at the most. And then we can enjoy the rest of the trip."

"Maybe," Tia said without enthusiasm. She had been thinking that so far as she was concerned, it wouldn't matter if she never went any place else. She was where she had always wanted to be and so far Morrow more than fulfilled her expectations.

"Is Simon or anyone else young going along?"

"Nope. You have to be twenty-one usually."

"Maybe, since you *want* to go and I don't, maybe I could talk Ashira into just taking you?" She felt guilty saying it, and Rabbit's reaction made her feel worse. He looked over at her in the dusk. "Maybe," he said, but he sounded hurt. "If you really don't want to go *that* bad!"

"But what?"

"Nothing," his voice was hardly audible. "If you don't go, I don't want to go either. It's no fun if there's nobody to share it with."

"Everybody else will be there."

"It's not the same—it's not you. They never lived there. And they've all been on these trips lots of times. They won't get very excited about anything. I'd be the only person who isn't grown up—and besides, we've been together a long time now—I'd be lonesome without you." He slid over next to her on the steps and slipped his hand over hers. "Even if you don't have to, please come along?"

She couldn't resist a plea like that, and Rabbit was too dear to her. "Okay," she said, "I didn't really think you'd want to go alone." She put her arm around his shoulder and hugged him.

"Then you'll go?"

"Yes. But I'm afraid."

"I think you should let Ashira know how much you're scared," he said. "She could probably fix it."

"No." Tia was firm. "I don't want anybody else to know."

For the past fifteen minutes or more Varas's group had been repeating the same eight bars, each time making a mistake and having to go back over it.

"I like that piece when it's played right," Rabbit commented. "There's one part that always makes me shiver when I hear it."

Tia obligingly, if a bit flatly, hummed the melody for him. "Did that make you shiver?"

"No," he said, but not wanting to insult her, added, "but it made my nose itch a little." And she punched him.

Much as she wanted to, Tia couldn't hold back the days. The morning of departure arrived and again the Morrowans thronged the dock to see the *Simone II* set sail. Unlike the ship's homecoming this was a somber occasion.

On the commons stood a tall monument which bore the names of eight hundred seventy-eight voyagers, all of whom had perished on Expeditions.

Some died by drowning, or in falls, in salvage or mining accidents, by earthquakes and landslides. But most were killed by the ruins of the old civilization. They died when sturdy-looking walls collapsed on top of them, when what was once a street sank into the transit tunnel beneath it, when aerial tramway pylons went down like dominoes. Before all vehicles were fitted with geiger counters, death by radiation from hot waste buried centuries before was not uncommon. Nor was poisoning by polluted water. In all these ways and more the Past threatened. Each time an expedition sailed, there was a good chance that not every member would return.

Although everyone could remain in mental contact for several days more at least, when the time came for actual physical leave-taking, many cried. Tia and Rabbit were among them.

Saying good-bye to people they cared about was something they had never done before. They found it very difficult. When the loading ramp started to retract and water could be seen between ship and jetty, Tia wanted very much to jump ship and swim to shore. But she didn't. She stood with the others at the rail, waving down at Max and Simon, Foran and Liane, everyone's faces blurred by the tears in her eyes until distance blurred them completely. At the harbor entrance the *Simone II* blew three blasts of farewell that echoed back and back again before she turned northwest and the peninsula blotted Morrow from view.

It was after 2 a.m., a moonless night. The *Simone II* was cruising north in waters just off the continental shelf at a point almost equidistant from the ancient sites of Los Angeles and San Diego. Her green running lights were on, their reflections swallowed up by the night waves until, slowly, the green reflected upon green and the waves were stilled.

They smelled it before they realized what it was. The odor crept into the intake ventilators and permeated all compartments with the evil pervasiveness of old drains. Within minutes there was a low hum of irritated human activity on board.

Tia was awakened by the low urgency of Varas's voice in the next compartment. There was an answering murmur of a woman's voice, too soft to distinguish. Before she had time to puzzle over what it meant there was a polite crackle as the ship's intercom came on. The captain's voice was a near whisper.

"Will you who are awake please see that all vent fans are turned to exhaust. We've switched to emergency filtration. The smell should clear out in ten minutes or so." There was a pause and Ashira's voice could be heard in the background, then Mark resumed speaking, "There is nothing to worry about. We're passing through a patch of algae—the

[64]

stuff we commonly call The Slime Mold. It's not supposed to grow this far out. But then it's not supposed to grow like this at all. I repeat, there is nothing to worry about. Just switch your fans to exhaust and go back to sleep."

Tia yawned, got out of bed and did as directed, then staggered back, slid under the blanket again and pulled it over her nose. Rabbit turned over with a thump and went back into deep sleep. Tia looked over, half hoping he might wake up and want to talk. She thought she was awake now. Something about the smell had revived old memories and she didn't want to be alone in the dark with them.

The door to the passageway opened noiselessly and Varas came in to check the heating/cooling unit. Seeing it on exhaust he silently queried, "Tia?" and finding her still awake but on the verge of bad dreams sat down on the end of her bed. "That part of your life is over, Tia. It can never come back. Except in dreams. When you see the Base again from your new perspective you will be better able to accept what I say. You were powerless and alone before. You won't ever be alone again—unless it is a privacy of your own choosing. I do not promise that you won't ever feel pain or grief. You will. Sometimes it is hard to live. But you are loved, both you and Rabbit, and we won't let anything bad happen to you."

"You won't make us stay at the Base—leave us behind?"

"You thought we might?" He was horrified. "You poor child—No!"

"Promise?"

"Promise." He reached out in the dimness and took her hand and held it between his two hands for a moment. Then rising, he whispered, "Tuck in your arm," and as she obediently did so he tucked the blanket around her shoulders.

"You go back to sleep now. It's a long time till morning," and laid his hand briefly against her cheek. Turning he tucked Rabbit's covers up more securely and then left the room as silently as he had entered.

The next morning, Tia and Rabbit were having breakfast when the ship shuddered twice, wallowed, and then became strangely still.

"Power's off," someone said the obvious.

"We're still coasting."

"Did we collide with something?"

Tia stood up and looked out the porthole by their table. Nothing had changed outside.

"What is it?"

"Nothing I can see."

"Let's go out on deck!" Rabbit said excitedly, but he had presence of mind to cram his two remaining sausages into his remaining bran muffin before running to the door.

"You're not going to eat out there, are you?" The idea revolted Tia.

Where she had been plowing through it a few

moments before, the ship now drifted in what appeared to be an ocean of green velvet. It surrounded her on all sides as far as the eye could see. It was an algaic substance resembling a thickly curded mold. The surface growth sent up long hairlike green cells while below the waterline it was an ugly brown. The pressure of the *Simone*'s bulk passing through it caused it to emit the stench of ancient effluvium. All morning almost no one had come out on deck because of the foul odor.

Now they were all out.

"Don't be alarmed," Jemmel's reassuring voice came from the P.A. system. "Our screws are fouled. We are going to anchor and reverse them to get this crud off. But, divers, I feel it only fair to warn you—you may have to go down and clean it off manually. So don't eat breakfast if you haven't yet." There was an ornery chuckle in his voice.

"Poor things." Tia was instantly sympathetic. The thought of entering physically into that foulness was repellent. She saw Rabbit look at his sandwich and then go over and put it into the waste barrel.

"When we regain power we will be heading west until we outrun the problem," Jemmel continued. "We are already twenty-five miles further out than we were on the last trip."

"Is it possible we are spreading the stuff?" Ashira wanted to know.

While the adults debated this possibility, Tia leaned over the rail and looked down. It was as if the ship was sunk into a deep carpet. Water was visible only at the very line of contact. The weight of the growth had stilled the waves to a hardly visible swell. The smell of the stuff and the slight heave of the ship communicated itself to her stomach.

"I'm going in now," she announced and ran for the nearest lavatory. There was a waiting line and she raced for her own compartment.

11

During the day the observation lounge was generally a lovely room of blue and green, illuminated by the constantly flickering light of the sun filtering through the waves above the heavy quartz bubble window. Tia and Rabbit were fond of the room; they spent many hours each day down here, watching the sea floor sliding past far beneath them, dotted here and there with small life, and kelplike plants waving in the current.

But today, the room was so dim that only the pencil lights on the base of the sofas illuminated it. The color reflecting through the waves was that of stale coffee.

"Why did we come down here?" Rabbit asked when they walked in and dropped with boredom onto the nearest lounge. "There's nothing to see in here."

"It's as good as any place today. I'm tired of staying in our room. I'm tired of reading. I'm tired of learning things—and we can only play so much ping pong and chess. And since we can't go out on deck—there's not much we can do."

The hull shook as the screws reversed, trying to shake loose the algae befouling them. Then the motors shut off.

"Look at that stuff floating up past the window," said Rabbit. "Gag!"

Minute particles of brown matter drifted by the pane, floating up to join the mass above the viewing port. Long wispy things like very fine rootlets trailed down along the glass from the growth.

"Did you see that?" Tia sat up and pointed.

"What?"

"It looked like a light."

"Probably a wave broke through and the sun pierced down."

"It didn't look like sun."

"Maybe there are divers in the water."

"Maybe . . . there it is again. It's blue. Do the divers carry blue lights?"

"No, very white lights."

"Besides, they would have had to go down when the motors were still running." Her mind sought Varas's and she relayed the blue lights. The response she got surprised her. It was sheer delight mixed with curiosity. "He's coming down to see," she reported to Rabbit.

"Who?"

"Varas."

"Oh? It flashed again—but it seems further out. It's hard to tell with all this junk in front of the glass."

If it had not been for the revolting appearance of the stuff they would have pressed their faces against the bulge of the glass in order to see more clearly. But the main charm of the observation window was its ability to make the viewer feel he was in the ocean—and to be in the midst of what was outside that glass at the moment wasn't an appealing thought, so they kept their distance and peered into the murk, waiting for Varas to arrive.

Which he did very shortly. Running, in fact. "Let's put out these lights. They may be giving back a reflection off the glass." He switched off even the stair light outside, then came to join the children. But unlike them, he got up as close to the glass as he possibly could.

"What do you think it is?" whispered Tia.

"I won't commit myself yet," thought Varas as a hint for complete silence. "Where was it the last time you saw it?"

"Right over there," Rabbit pointed.

For minutes the only sound in the room was that of their breathing and the gentle whisper of the ventilation system. Nothing happened in the murk outside. Rabbit got tired of being still for so long and shifted restlessly and Tia sympathized with him.

Then the light show began—a flick here, a flash there, an answering flash from several yards further out. All the lights seemed to be several yards below them in depth and muted by the scum in the water. "What is it?" wondered Tia.

"Bioluminescence," came Varas's answer. "Light emitted by living things."

"What things? What's out there?"

"Probably no more than algaic plankton, but possibly some sea creature or creatures."

"Fish? Where would they come from? I thought the ocean's fish all died?"

"The deep . . ." he began, then remembering

their ignorance, "Imagine we are in a ship capable of submerging to unlimited depths," he suggested. He flashed them an image of a clean ocean as seen through a viewport such as this. In his imagined picture, light dappled the surface waves like a liquid ceiling right above their heads. Still in the grip of his imagination they sank slowly until light from the surface dimmed. Colors faded—red, orange, and yellow disappeared. "Two hundred feet down," he noted.

At six hundred feet all they could see was deep blue—the same shade of blue as in those flashes outside. Slowly all light, all color faded and there was only blackness, silence and deep cold.

"I cannot make you feel the pressure from the weight of the water above at this depth. It would crush a man to the thickness of tissue paper. Nor have I seen what I shall show you next. Only read and dreamed of it."

The image of blackness returned and then was spattered by starbursts of colored lights. "These were the fishes of the deep, all equipped with bioluminescent organs. And, according to the ancient marine researchers, the deeper the water, the more spectacular the display of colors."

"How deep is the ocean?" asked Tia.

"At its deepest, seven miles. In the depths the vast slow currents creep from pole to pole through endless night. They carry with them dissolved oxygen and food in infinite particles—food and oxygen such as this growth outside the window provides. We find it disgusting, but it may contribute more to the Balance of Life than Morrow could ever hope to."

His mind had leaped beyond their understanding and they waited for him to return.

"It is possible some of those deep-layer creatures survived—perhaps those below one thousand feet where pressure kept the oxygen and nutrients in suspension. And those capable of enduring less pressure rise to feed in the dimness of this growth. Our ship is still—the hull vibrations its crew produces minimal. We may be seeing creatures long believed extinct—or new creatures. I must record this if we can."

He hurried off to get a camera.

Tia sat spellbound watching the light show outside. It seemed to her that if she let her imagination help, she could see a dim outline of a moving mass out there. But it wasn't her imagination that the lights were moving closer. Rabbit sat up slowly and like herself, almost quit breathing in anticipation. Closer and closer the lights came and then suddenly a tubular mass stretched across the center of the bubble window.

"Look!"

Rabbit's excited yell of amazement told her she was not imagining anything. These lights were all on one creature. And at that cry from Rabbit, it turned toward them one large flat eye, its disc outlined by five tiny blue lights. With a frightened flick of its flesh it seemed to contract and sink like a lead weight below the viewport. A second later the water outside had turned black.

12

"Possibly a variety of *Perichthys* or a deep realm unclassified squid," Varas repeated the computer's guesses. "Out of their recorded biotope and in an enlarged form. Whatever it was—I missed it! I chose that moment to go for a camera."

He was so disappointed that Tia felt sorry for him. "Maybe it'll come back?" she said to give him hope.

"Not with divers down. With all that fuss it's probably a mile beneath us now and five miles out."

"But at least you know another species exists," Ashira reminded him. "That in itself is quite remarkable. Where there is one, there are others. It didn't appear spontaneously."

"True." He brightened. "But you know—it might possibly be a variety of *Aequorea*." He showed the children what he imagined the bioluminescent jellyfish to look like. "Fascinating creature—and with abrupt movement a dangling tentacle mass might look like the thing you described."

"But the eye?" questioned Ashira.

"There was an eye!" Rabbit said in case anyone doubted it. "I saw it too. A big black smart-looking eye! Huh, Tia?"

"I wonder why we haven't seen them before?"

"Perhaps because we knew that officially they

didn't exist—and disregarded what we saw," said Ashira. "Tia and Rabbit are not blinded by such preconception."

The ship began to hum faintly with vibration as the generators came on. Then the vibration increased and the propellers began to spin again. The dark water outside grew opaque with particles and the ship moved forward. Ten miles west she ran clear of the algae and into open sea. Ten miles beyond that she turned north again to reach landfall late that night off what had once been called San Francisco Bay.

The following day was spent in preparation for the landing party. Solar absorption panels were fitted atop all four amphibians. To add to their purely functional appearance, the lower paneling on each car had been removed and half-tracks put on for rough terrain. For emergency power, fuel cells were installed and the cars stripped of all unnecessary weight. Cameras and recorders were given last minute checks, as was all specimen collection equipment. Camping supplies had been packed at Morrow into the three units which would make the actual trek into the interior. The fourth car would remain with the ship as taxi transport between ship and shore—or as a rescue vehicle if that became necessary.

Tia watched all this activity with a mixture of fascination and unease. The fear came from her inability to shake off the dread of their destination.

The fascination was with all the preparation. And as she watched crate upon crate of foodstuffs being loaded, she began to smile. Rabbit caught her thought.

"It is funny, huh? We came all the way down to the sea with two rabbits and some dried apples in a leather sack."

"I wouldn't want to do it again," Tia said, "but I kind of enjoyed parts of that trip—being on our own for the first time, seeing new places."

"Especially being on our own," agreed Rabbit.

"The Expediton Party will dine at 6 p.m.," the captain's voice announced on the intercom. "At that time final instructions will be given. Please do not be late."

A separate long table had been set up for the eighteen members of the expedition and as soon as everyone was finished eating, Ashira got down to business. On the table before her was a chart.

"We went over this chart as we loaded this morning. Several items were missing then. Pat, did you locate your missing socket set?"

"No, but Jemmel found a spare in the ship's stores. It's in my tool box."

"Tom—the portable lights?"

"In Car Three."

"Good."

She went on down her check list calling off names and things forgotten or not ready until the last minute. After twenty minutes or so Rabbit was

EXPEDITION: #82   Sailing: 3/1/97

INITIATOR: A. Morrow, R. E.

DESTINATION: Lat. _____ Long. _____

PURPOSE: Contact — Observation — Reconnaissance

Car	Staff	Capacity/Assignment	Freight Carried
1	Mark Santini	Exp. Leader/Driver/LC	Tents, Shovels, Pails
			Pots, Pans
	David Suimoto	Chief Navigator/Guard	Food Cartons
			Medical Kit
	Patricia Chenot	Mechanic	2 Pistols
			1 Stun Gun
	Henri Chenot	Mechanic	1 Flare Gun
			Tool Box
	Luiz Rameriz	Botanical Geneticist	2 Jacks
			1 Set of Treads
	Deirdre Darcy	Zoologist/Guard	Maps
			Personal Gear
2	Ashira Morrow	Driver/Biochemist/LC	Tents, Shovels, Pails
			Food Cartons
	Varas Morrow	Anthropologist/Navigator/LC	Powersaw
			1 Pickax
	Tia Morrow	Guide/Interpreter	2 Rock Hammers
			1 Core Kit
	Rabbit Morrow	Guide/Interpreter/LC	Cameras/recorders
			Medical Supplies
	Lora Sandis	Physician	1 Flare Gun
			2 Pistols
	Tom Li	Cinematographer	Pump and Hoses
			2 Spare Wheels
			Maps
			Personal Gear
3	Saidia Sandis	Driver/Empathyst	Tents, Stove, Food
			Cartons
	Malcolm Kim	Records/Navigator	Lab Kits
			2 Jacks, Shovels, Pails
	Elaine Balchan	Senior Geneticist/LC	Specimen Packs
			1 Collecting Net
	Ivan Kahn	Senior Chef/Records	2 Collapsible Cages
			2 Spare Tires
	Sophia Wu	Still Photography	Medical Kit
			1 Flare Gun
	Don Lloyd	Lab Tech/Guard	1 Set of Treads
			Photographer's Lights
			Maps
			Personal Gear

squirming in his seat, bored with details. Ashira shot him a quick private message. "You can leave whenever you wish, or sit still." He blushed to his ears and subsided. Tia saw him blush and wondered why but he wouldn't tell her.

"I've been wondering, since this is our first contact with other people, shouldn't we be taking along gifts? It would make a great scene." Tom liked his documentaries to have drama.

"Giving beads to the natives?" Elaine was being sarcastic and she glanced briefly at Tia to see what her reaction would be. Tia didn't understand the allusion, just the faint contempt in the woman.

"That's exactly the attitude we don't want, Elaine," Varas said. "We are not going to repeat past history if we can help it."

"That's idealistic twaddle," Elaine judged it. "Just seeing us will alter their culture. They'll probably think we're gods."

"No," Tia disagreed. "If he's anything, their god is something dark and scary and loud. You're too clean and quiet. They won't even think you're strong enough to be dangerous. But they might worship the cars."

"That *is* primitive," Elaine sneered.

"No," answered Tia. "That is ignorance."

Ashira smiled. It pleased her to see that her protégé wasn't intimidated by Elaine. "In any event," she said, "all this is purely speculative. There will be no gifts. Back to practical matters. Mark, would you please go over the route once more. Tia and Rabbit, you can tell us what you remember of the terrain as we go along. Remember that we have to consider the cars. Are there heavy woods, deep mud, canyons, etc.?"

It was after eight by the time the briefing ended. While the expedition members would sleep on board that last night, the three amphibians were to be taken to the beach for final loading there. One by one they were driven onto the hydraulic hoist and let down slowly to water level inside the center hull. The double doors at the water line hissed open, a sliding ramp angled down into the water, and the cars clanked off into the waves.

From the top deck, Tia and Rabbit watched. It made her feel better to see them—so jaunty and sure of themselves in the open sea. Their running lights shone like the center jewels in the tiara of white wake gleaming in the dusk. One by one the cars pulled up on the beach and parked above the tideline.

"We'll be there in two days." Rabbit's voice sounded very small.

"You scared too?"

"A little."

"Yeah. I wish it was over. I don't want to see them."

"I d-do. But maybe not enough to go there."

"You're not going to have nightmares, are you?" It was almost a threat.

"N-not anymore than you," said Rabbit.

"Let's go ask Ashira if she'll soothe us before we go to sleep. When she does that, I don't remember anything." Tia did not miss the fact that Rabbit had stuttered again, something he had not done for weeks.

They found Ashira still in the dining room with Varas, Elaine, and most of the expedition. When Ashira saw them coming back she sensed what they wanted, excused herself, and came over to walk them to their room. While they got ready for bed she told them stories of her own childhood, silly stories to make them laugh, and when each was finally under the covers, she tucked them in and went on talking until their minds reached the first dream state. Then her level of concentration shifted, intensified, focused on their consciousness and blurred it past their own dreaming.

Tia was aware of a floating sensation, as if her mind alone had entered a state of free fall with no beginning and no end. She was part of Rabbit and Ashira and Varas and all life that had ever been or ever would be. For a brief moment she understood mind unending. Her breathing became as slow and even as her pulse and she slept.

It was raining when they set off in the morning, a fine wind-blown drizzle that immediately made Tia's short hair friz. There was no need to say goodbye to Jemmel or anyone who remained aboard. They would be close enough so all could remain in telepathic contact throughout the trip. Their duffle kits had already been taxied to the beach and tucked under their assigned seats. All Tia and Rabbit had to do to begin the final step of this journey was get into the taxi.

They sat in the back and through the rear window watched the *Simone II* grow smaller in the distance. With the coolness outside, the pane fogged from the heat of the passengers. The front windshield wipers squeaked across the glass. Everybody sat lost in their private little world. Not a word was spoken all the way to shore.

The rest of the party was waiting for them. Standing around the cars in their hooded rainproofs with visors they looked like animated chessmen.

"Let's go," Ashira called as she got out of the taxi amphibian. "The sooner we're away from the coast, the better our chances of getting away from the rain," and without looking back at the mother ship, she climbed into the driver's seat of the second car.

Mark led the three-car caravan along the beach for several miles before they came to the first landmark Tia recognized.

"There's the pine woods we ran through when we saw the sea for the first time!" She pointed out the rain-streaked window. "If you go through there, it will lead you to a lot of ruins along a river. You can't see the end of them."

"M-mountains of them!" said Rabbit. "Really old ones."

"No," Varas corrected him. "These ruins are the same age as all the rest. They look older due to repeated earthquakes. Several violent seismic shocks hit this coast sometime in the 2300s—at the same time the Japanese islands were devastated. Parts of the coast sank seven to twelve feet while the Chilean Andes rose an equal amount. Tidal waves leveled much of this area. Some of these mountains are not ruins, but real mountains covered with debris. This area to the south was once a hilly city."

Ashira turned right and followed Mark up a grassy dune toward the trees. Behind them Saidia dropped back to allow space in case the lead cars had to slow or detour at the tree line.

"We won't chance going through the trees if

David can find a better route," Mark decided. "I'm heading north toward the river mouth. It's high tide. There may be enough water over the mud flats to allow passage. With as much weight as we're carrying, I'd hate to get stuck."

"We're not going through the trees?" Tia saw the lead car veer away.

"They're too thick—too close together for the cars to clear," Ashira replied.

"Oh."

"We f-found our first avocado tree b-back there. Remember?" said Rabbit twisting in his seat to look back. "I've liked them ever since."

"I noticed," Varas said dryly.

The car hummed faintly to itself as they rolled along. Its treads crunched snail shells and slapped sand against the hull with lulling regularity. Ashira and Saidia followed Mark's trail so closely that the tracks left in the sand suggested but one heavy vehicle had passed this way—for only the second time in centuries.

They rounded a spit of sand jutting down into the water, passed the massive block of what must have once been a bridge abutment and saw to the east the wide slow mouth of the estuary, beyond that ruins and in the distance, mountains. What had once been a deep harbor port was now a swampy salt flat through which the force of the river had cut a channel deeper than the rest. It was up this channel the cars traveled.

Their speed was slow, partly to conserve power and utilize the force of the incoming tide, and partly because of the danger of submerged wrecks. Once in the river the tall marsh grasses on the mudflats loomed high above them for mile after mile, shutting out any side views.

"Are you *sure* this is the same place Rabbit and I saw?" Tia asked after long minutes had passed. "I don't see anything familiar."

They assured her it was. The marshy growth diminished at about the same time the skeletal remains of chemical storage tanks appeared on the left bank and beyond them the support towers of a long gone bridge stretched across the swamp.

"Th-there it is!" Rabbit pointed excitedly to the south toward the ruined city sprawling across the hills.

"Could we pause here?" asked Tom. "I want some footage of this." Ashira flipped on the rear flashers and coasted to a drift. Behind Saidia followed suit. By law, on any expedition which the Elite accompanied, the Elite's car must never be passed but kept always between at least two vehicles. Tom pressed a button and a window slid down. He aimed the camera and it began to whine.

"Once at least six million people lived within view of where we sit," Varas mused. "More millions in the hills and valleys nearby. Ships from around the world docked in this swamp. The air roared with the noise of people, aircraft, surface vehicles, tube traffic, ships' horns. Listen now." He waved toward the surroundings. All that could be heard was the idling slurry of the amphibians' props.

"How m-many is six million?"

"Too many!" said Lora.

It was more than Tia could imagine or wanted to. Unlike Rabbit, who was excited by the ruins, she found them oppressive, as if they were still haunted with the fear of that distant past.

"Mark's getting too far ahead. We'll have to go on," Ashira told Tom as she eased back into gear and resumed power.

Tia watched the ruins slide by on both banks now as they headed east. The river grew narrower, deeper. They left the ocean behind them. Gradually grass and trees began to appear again and all trace of humans was gone. The river gained enough current to push against the amphibians. Mark left the water and led them to the clearly visible slash of an ancient roadway through the hills. The grass grew in clumps on the roadbed's flatness and the caravan bounced along, winding its way around the occasional tree or manzanita thicket. Rabbits hopped away unconcerned to see the cars pass, but the pigs flushed from the thickets obviously regarded the cars as dangerous enemies.

They camped in mid afternoon by the edge of a wide lake. The rain and wind had stopped, but fog limited visibility to less than one thousand yards. The lingering clouds had cut off the sun's radiation and the storage cells were low.

"I don't want to switch to emergency cells unless

we have to," Mark decided. "With the weight we're carrying, they'd only last an hour or so anyhow. Provided we were going in the right direction."

"And I don't want the added thrill of seeing you drive off a cliff in the fog," said Ashira. "The sun should be back tomorrow."

Tia and Rabbit were glad to be stopping.

"I g-guess it's good to be able to ride when you're going a long way," said Rabbit as he got out. "But it's dull. All you c-can do is sit and look. Nothing happens to you that way."

"I'm glad you feel the need of activity," said Ivan the cook. "You and Tia can help me gather some wood—if we can find anything dry."

After a few minutes of stretching their legs, everyone set to work. There were sanitation pits to be dug and tents to be set up over them, a shower tent and sleeping tents to erect, a fire pit to be dug, water to be fetched.

The damp air magnified sounds; Tia and Rabbit could hear the camp makers in the background as they wandered along the lake shore collecting wood. There was plenty of wood, much of it pushed into piles by the waves of past storms. The only problem, aside from its being damp, was that the driftwood tangles harbored hordes of mosquitoes. Since their clothing protected all but their face and hands, it was there the bugs landed and in minutes both of them had welts.

"Kachoo! Ka-kachoo!" Tia sneezed repeatedly as a mosquito went up her nose.

"Boy, you sure forget about m-mosquitoes fast when you don't have to p-put up with them," observed Rabbit. He slapped himself and the offending insects left bloody smears on his cheek.

"I didn't miss them at all," said Tia. "Let's get as much wood as we can carry and get back to camp."

But when they reached camp, the situation was no better. As if starved for human companionship, the mosquitoes had arrived in clouds almost as thick as the mental distress the campers were radiating.

"What did they eat before we arrived?" Ivan wanted to know.

"I don't know," said Lora, "but I'm going to check them for malaria."

There were no trypanosomes; the mosquitoes were clean. Merely pesky. Repellent proved largely ineffective and the idea of exposing any more skin than necessary to their rapacious appetites cut the number of showers taken that night to two—Ashira and Saidia. Using the sanitation tent couldn't be avoided by anyone and resulted in much discreet scratching.

"Do you remember the mosquitoes being this bad?" Ashira asked.

"Oh, yes," said Tia, "especially in spring."

"You never mentioned them."

Tia shrugged. "I guess we just took them for granted."

"Oh," said Ashira, and wondered what other unpleasantness they had "taken for granted."

14

The wind rose before dawn and swept the mosquitoes away with the clouds. In her tent, Tia woke groggy and grumpy. Like all but the heaviest sleepers, she had spent much of the night tense and listening for the next maddening whine of a mosquito buzzing her ear.

The wind buffeted gently against the tent. Through the low window she could see mountain peaks gleaming snow-bright in the sun's rays. There were stealthy footsteps in the wet grass as someone passed the back of the tent. She heard a car door open and metal clank lightly on metal. Someone was up and working but trying not to waken anyone else, she thought.

She eased out of her sleeping bag, silently picked up a change of clothes from her pack and crawled to the tent door. Outside she stood erect beneath the tent flap and surveyed the morning. Heavy dew silvered the grass and tents. Drops sparkled on the amphibians. No one else was in sight. The silence seemed odd to her, no roosters crowed, no birds sang. The bushes whispered when the wind brushed them and the lake lapped its shore. Without the fog, the lake view looked familiar to her and then she realized with a sense of shock that it was the same lake she and Rabbit had camped beside. They were getting closer.

Hoping activity would still the butterflies in her stomach, she headed toward the toilet and shower. The little fuel cell had kept the water tepid through the night and when she emerged from the shower, she felt much better. Ashira was right, she decided as she walked along. Not having a bath before going to bed affected your personality.

There was still no one else up. The fire pit was cold. She raked out the ashes and looked about for the hatchet Ivan had left in the log he'd used as a chopping block. The hatchet was gone. Thinking he'd put it in out of the damp, she went over to the No. 3 amphibian to get it. It wasn't readily visible.

She shrugged and was about to close the car door again when it struck her that the inside of the car looked very messy. As if someone else had been hunting something they couldn't find and had lost patience. Mark would be irked if he saw that. She straightened things up as best she could and went over to Ashira's car to get the hatchet in the car tool box.

When the fire was burning brightly, she filled two coffee pots with lake water and put them on to perk, then opened the dry food chest to get herself some bread to toast. The bread was gone, all of it, along with the box of dough Ivan had packed to bake on the journey. For a moment she was simply confused. Who would have moved it? For what reason? The box was weatherproof, nothing would spoil . . .

There was the branch-cracking sound of a large animal moving in the bushes on the other side of the cars. Probably pigs, she thought glancing that way, her mind still on the missing food. What she saw made the hair rise on her arms. It was the bobbing heads of three men running through the brush.

Within seconds of her alarm, the entire camp was in an uproar. Her images had blurted right into the sleeping minds of the other seventeen, not only alerting them, but searing them with her fear.

Tom was the first to emerge from his tent clad only in his shorts but clutching his camera. "Which way?" he wanted to know and ran off after the fleeing men.

"Base men?" Ashira wanted confirmation and at the same time chided herself and Mark for not thinking to post a guard.

"They never came this far before," Tia said, feeling that she and Rabbit might somehow be held responsible for this.

"They're probably still hunting for the Major's party," was Varas's opinion. "Finding us was an accident."

"Deirdre, where's your stun gun?" Mark demanded of the zoologist, and the two of them took off after Tom and his quarry.

"They could have bashed in our heads while we slept," Elaine reminded everyone. "They had the hatchet to do it with. And, doubtless, the mentality.

These aren't wild animals we're tracking, they're men—throwbacks to the old species. We've got to remember what we're dealing with." She was just warming to the subject when Ashira unceremoniously ordered her silent.

Rabbit came running, wanting to know if Tia recognized them.

"I just saw the backs of their heads," she told him.

"L-let's go s-see," he said, grabbing her hand and trying to tug her with him.

"You'll stay here," said Varas. "It's far too dangerous."

In a few minutes, Mark and the others returned. They brought with them the sacks of bread dough, two shovels, and three pails. "They dropped them," he said. "We'd better check inventory to see if they have any weapons other than the hatchet."

"Did you see them?" Ashira asked.

"No. Tom did. They're hidden in the low mounds up ahead here. I didn't want anybody to walk into an ambush. So we came back."

"Good. Let's have breakfast, pack up, and get underway. We're approximately fifty miles from their village. It will take them at least two days to walk back and report our presence. We want to beat them home and avoid a possible reception committee."

"If you cross the lake and head up the river, that's probably the fastest way," said Tia. "Yeah," agreed Rabbit. "We k-know the way that way. When you c-come to a bunch of big square st-stones in the river bed, you h-head to the Path again."

"That sounds like bridge foundations for the roadway," said David, the navigator. "Let me get my maps. Do you remember the terrain from the river to your village?"

"Kind of," said Tia.

"Can the amphibian follow the route you took? Is it heavily wooded?" He was remembering the diary of the first Morrowan to discover the Base. He had left his car at the river and walked in.

Tia wasn't sure. "There were lots of bare spots," she said, "lots of places full of clay mounds near the Path, but I never looked at them with the idea of whether a car could get through. Maybe if we cut some trees."

"We'll just have to wait and see."

An hour later they set off across the lake. From a hillock on the shore behind them three men watched them go and the men's eyes were bright with fear.

15

They covered those last fifty miles in five hours. The
river was a good highway although its recurrent
sand banks required much shifting and maneuvering by the drivers. When the river angled north,
they went overland, sometimes on old road beds,
sometimes cross-country. They traveled constantly
uphill, but at a pace so gradual the increased elevation went unnoticed by the passengers. Tia felt
lightheaded but didn't mention it, thinking the
cause of her discomfort was fear.

The nearer they came, the more familiar the view
of the hills and distant mountains, the quieter she
and Rabbit grew. "In a few days it will all be over,"
she kept telling herself. "I can stand it till then." And
in less organized fashion she considered alternately
how impressed those Base people were going to be
when they saw her now, how sorry they would be
that they had been mean to her and Rabbit, and how
scared she was at the whole idea of seeing any of
them again.

"It's getting close in here." Varas opened a
window.

"If mosquitoes are out there, I'd prefer lack of air
to the bites," said Lora.

But there were no mosquitoes. Nor did opening

the window relieve the lessened oxygen problem.

"It's the elevation," Ashira reminded them. "We are three thousand feet above sea level." She glanced over at Varas. "You take it easy up here." There was concern in her voice. "Before The Death of the Seas one had to go above ten thousand feet to find air this thin."

"We're getting close now," said Tia. "I used to hunt pebbles in those mounds over there."

"How deep is the woods beyond?"

"Pretty wide. If you go that way," she pointed southwest, "you can circle around and come into the fields by a creek. We might have to cut some trees, but I think we can get through—huh, Rabbit?"

"Or we can go up to where we . . . where the Base gets the salt—but that's k-kind of rough and hilly."

"I don't know that way," said Tia.

Ashira checked with Mark and the caravan turned southwest. Brush slapped against the sides of the cars and the briars they crushed beneath them scratched under the hull. The screws were up as high as they could go and still it was necessary to stop several times to free them from a grasping bush.

"Start going left now," directed Rabbit. "I think we're p-pretty close to the creek."

The caravan dipped and bumped over the rough terrain, weaving around tall old pines and finally lurching down toward the creek, which could be seen intermittently gleaming through the foliage. Then the lead car nosed into the creek bed and

turned east. Ashira gave an unconscious sigh of
relief. Even if the water wasn't deep enough to float
the vehicle, the gravel stream bed provided an easier
road to drive than the past ten miles overland had
been.

At the edge of the woods, the scraggly fields of the
Base opened before them. As soon as she saw the
ragged stubble of last year's corn, Tia's chest
tightened uncomfortably.

One by one the amphibians lurched up the creek
bank and out onto the field where they came to a
halt. A band of women was working with mattocks
and picks, trying to dig out stumps in a new clearing.
They stood less than fifty yards from where the cars
emerged into sight. Slowly, as if not believing what
they saw, one by one the women stopped work and
turned to stare. There was no shouting, no running.
They stood like wild things. Waiting.

"Don't let them see your cameras," Varas warned
Tom and Sophia. "They might mistake them for
weapons and be frightened."

"Everyone stay in the cars," Ashira ordered.

"Did I ever look like that?" Tia wondered as she
stared at them. At this distance, in their still pose, the
women's faces were blurs, one indistinguishable
from the other. All had the same wild, tangled hair.
All wore the same sacklike brown leather dress.
Their feet and arms were bare and muddy. But it
wasn't their bedraggledness that bothered her so
much as their hangdog air of subjugation. She had

not been so aware of it before, and seeing it now, and remembering, disturbed her.

"How—uh—small they are," the doctor said, as if feeling the need to break the silence in the car. For a moment no one answered and all kept their thoughts to themselves.

Tia wondered what Dr. Lora was really thinking and she blushed with shame to imagine what the Morrowans' original impressions of her must have been. Would they think less of her and Rabbit now that they saw where they came from? What they came from?

"It's hard to keep clean here," she said, "especially when you have to work so hard."

"Be-besides, n-nobody here c-cares about dirt," Rabbit's stutter was back in full force when he spoke.

"Can you pick up any reactions, Tia?" Ashira wanted to know.

It hadn't occurred to Tia to try, she was so self-absorbed. But when she focused on the women, she received almost nothing but vague apprehension. "It's as if they saw . . ." She couldn't find words or transfer impressions for what she received so she simply shared her reception.

"Odd," was Ashira's reaction. "They don't suspect we are human—or that we are separate from the cars. They see only three 'things.' "

"Can I get out?" asked Tia. "I want to see if they'll recognize me."

Rabbit giggled nervously. "With your h-hood up

and your sh-shades on, it's h-hard for me to re-recognize you."

"I'll take my shades off."

"That's not wise at this elevation. Your eyes have become used to protection," Lora warned.

"Try it, but stay close to the car," Ashira decided.

"Okay." Tia swung up the door slowly. As she did so the women and girls took a few cautious steps backward, but if they said anything, their words were lost in the distance. When she stepped down onto the soggy field there was an audible murmur of dismay. She paused for a moment and then walked slowly toward them.

"Don't be afraid," she called in the Base language. "We won't hurt you." No response. "It's me—Tia."

At that someone screamed and then screamed again. She thought it was her mother; she was receiving a familiar fear pattern. Other voices cried out and, as Tia kept walking, the women turned from her and fled in panic into the woods behind them.

Tia stood and watched them go and on her face was a look of disgust. "Why did that scare them?" she thought as she put her shades back on. "You'd think they'd at least remember my name and ask where I'd been all this time."

"Perhaps they did," suggested Ashira. "Perhaps they ran *because* they recognized you."

"Why. . . ." Tia started to ask and then answered

her own question. "Because they're still afraid of me?"

"And because they may have believed you dead."

"Yeah," said Rabbit. "S-so f-far as th-they know, wh-where could we g-go? Th-they must have th-thought we died."

"Get back in the car and we'll go up to the settlement," ordered Mark. "The screams drew an audience. People are standing up there by the buildings watching us."

"I w-wonder w-what th-they'll say to-to m-m-me?"

With the lugs of the halftracks throwing mud, the amphibians moved out across the fields toward the settlement. Conical stacks of hay and straw turned gray by weathering stood near the barns. Tall hardwoods in new leaf thrust above a tangle of shake-roofed log buildings. Over their roofs could be seen the crude stone square of the church bell tower in the center of the community.

As they approached the outbuildings a motley mixture of odors was sucked into the cars' ventilation systems. Aging cow manure, privies, garbage, woodsmoke—all these smells predominated over the usual scents of earth and grass. By unspoken consent all car windows went up and the air purifiers went on.

While the adults were silently revolted and wondering why all of this waste was not being properly utilized as fertilizer on these worn-out fields, Tia and Rabbit took the stink for granted.

The Base had always smelled like this. Instead they were looking back, watching to see if the women would come out of hiding now that the cars had gone. But the women did not reappear.

Mark was headed toward the widest approach to the center of the settlement, a point between barns and sheds where the biggest crowd of villagers had gathered. When the caravan reached that point, not a soul remained in sight. Ahead lay the open green around the cairnlike structure that was the Base church. "Do you think they're hiding in there?" he asked.

"No," said Tia, "the doors are shut. They wouldn't have had time to push them open. They're too heavy."

"Let's take advantage of their shyness to tour the village now while they're hiding," Ashira suggested. "If they turn hostile, we may not have the chance later."

"We'll do it by car," Mark ordered.

The ancient ancestors of the local people would not have been impressed by the appearance of the vehicles that now cautiously crept about their base. They had had vehicles almost as sophisticated and far more powerful. But all memory of that had long since faded from their descendants.

Their descendants lived in log houses whose rooftops were only slightly higher than these alien cars, and whose doors would make every adult Morrowan involuntarily bow to enter. Tia and

Rabbit pointed out the functions of each building.

"That L-shaped building is the mess hall—the kitchen's in the corner and the Fathers eat in the small end by themselves."

"The women's quarters, the infant house . . ."

"Stop here." The request was almost unanimous.

When Tia got out of the car, here in the village, she thought her knees were going to buckle. Rabbit caught her arm and said, "It's okay." She nodded stoically and tried to ignore the mute illogical terror that was making her heart pound.

As head guard, David went first, gun drawn, and pushed open the plank door of the infant house. From inside there was an "Ahh!" like an intake of breath and then a choked cry of fright. Tia heard the back door to the cabin slam and wondered who they'd scared off. An angry baby began to cry and two more joined in.

"No adults." Upon David's announcement, the visitors entered.

It was dark inside after the brightness of the sunlight. To Tia the room looked as it always had. On top of the low stone fireplace was what amounted to a big sand box, with the sand kept more or less warm and dry by the heat below. On the sand lay five tiny black-haired, black-eyed babies covered by rabbit pelts. The two who hadn't been crying now burst into tears at the sight of the intruders.

"Rough on skin but clever in a crude way," decided Lora. She gently rubbed a small leg and wondered at the skin texture. It was tougher than an adult Morrowan's skin. "They change the sand when it's soiled?"

"Yes," said Tia, thinking how frightened the babies must be to cry like that.

"Obviously not too often," Elaine wrinkled her nose and Tia wanted to kick her.

Varas leaned over the nursery to view the babies more closely and they screamed louder in a terrified quintet. "They appear healthy." He raised the coverlet, and then hastily dropped it.

"They're afraid of us," Rabbit said. "We look f-funny to th-them. I th-think it's the sunglasses."

"But I'm projecting comfort," Varas said, confused but apologetic. "Babies soothe easily."

"Not these babies," Tia reminded him. "They can't receive you."

"These platforms with the hay—who sleeps here?" Ashira took in the rest of the room with a sweep of her hand.

"The little kids—I s-slept here till we ran away," Rabbit said. "It's p-pretty warm if you all keep t-together. Except when the r-r-roof leaked."

"All the roofs leak," said Tia.

"Does any adult stay here at night?"

"No, they don't like the smell. Or the crying. These babies cry a lot more than yours."

"So would I," said Ashira and pushed her way past the others to the door.

As she watched Ashira leave, for some reason Tia

remembered the velvet box Simon had mentioned. She flashed the image to Rabbit and he nodded and smiled at her.

The Morrowans were no more impressed with the rest of the buildings they entered. They couldn't really understand why the people of the Base lived this way.

To her amazement, Tia found herself occasionally defending the villagers. "They don't *have* anything else," she said when asked why only rabbit hides were used as clothing and coverlets. "A cowhide can only belong to the Major."

"But the most primitive peoples could weave," Elaine said.

"And what would these people weave?" Tia asked. "They have no sheep—no cotton."

"As I recall, technology had made hand weaving a lost art by the twenty-first century," Varas mused. "Certainly one wouldn't expect to find a loom on a military base. Of course, they might reinvent it. They weave a fair basket. The ancient Hawaiians made cloth from bark."

The fireplaces also troubled the Morrowans. They could recognize the need for them, but the continuous smoke in the air morally offended them as much as the Fathers' custom of using everyone else as slaves.

The Morrowans did not inspect the Fathers' House, much to Tia and Rabbit's disappointment. The children had never been allowed in. A long building with tiny rooms opening off a central hall, the guards pronounced it too dangerous to enter without knowing what waited behind those closed doors, and not worth the trouble of finding out. After a brief tour of the Girls' House and some work sheds, the Morrowans returned to their cars.

They parked in a row in front of the church, the Elite's car flanked by the other two for protection. It was twenty after two in the afternoon.

16

As previously planned, the armed guards got out first, weapons in hand. They climbed to the top of the church where they had a clear view of the commons from all points. Fuel cells, rolls of fencing, poles, and insulators were unloaded. By five o'clock an electric fence surrounded the camp. Tiny red warning lights flashed from atop each fence pole. Two flood lights were mounted on the church roof.

"Well," Ashira noted as she surveyed the fence, "we've achieved security—at the cost of isolation."

"Wh-where do you think th-they went?" said Rabbit, referring to his Base kinsmen. Since the Morrowans entered the Base, there had been no further sight of the inhabitants.

"They'll return," said Varas. "Before they do, I want to look inside this place. They may not take kindly to strangers invading the sanctuary."

"Th-that's just the ch-church," said Rabbit. "I d-don't think th-they have a s-s-sanctuary."

"Possibly not," agreed Varas soberly.

The logs that propped shut the double door of the building were removed and the massive doors pulled open. There was a sour smell of old cement, torch smoke, and generations of unwashed people. The interior, filled with rows of split log benches, was separated by a center aisle. At the front of the room an ancient plastic table stood on a raised platform.

Tia had always been in awe of the church, always frightened to enter it. Now she saw it as a crude windowless meeting hall, smaller than she remembered. Beside her, Sophia was setting up a tripod to take photographs and Tom was setting up the portable lights. Tia wondered why. There were a million other things more interesting than this hole in the ground.

Mark shared Tia's reaction. "Is this it? A bench-filled warehouse?"

"B-but you h-haven't seen the Missile. Th-that's what makes it scary! Come on." Rabbit ran back along the wall to where a curtained door was visible in the dimness. "Oh, b-better bring tube-torches. It's d-dark down th-there."

"And air tanks," added Tia. "It's hard to breathe. Especially coming back up."

While Ashira and Mark went to get the equipment, Varas wandered about the room, inspecting the walls, examining the axe marks on the benches, checking to see how the legs had been pegged in at intervals. He kept shaking his head.

"What's wrong?" Tia asked him.

"The workmanship. It's functional, but so—awkward. When we finish here I must see their tool shop. They do have a forge?"

Tia and Rabbit looked at each other.

"Where do they smelt their metal?" He gave them a visual of a blacksmith's shop he'd seen in pictures. Both shook their heads. There wasn't such a thing at the Base.

"But they have axes—cutting instruments? Where do they come from?"

"They're mostly relics," said Tia. "Except for the stone hoes and things the women make."

"Where do they find the relics?"

Tia shrugged. "I don't know. I never thought about it. Ruins, probably.'

"Interesting. I do hope they get over their fear soon. I'd very much like to meet them."

Ashira returned with Mark, carrying two tube torches and three small oxygen tanks. "Mark will stand watch while we're below. He doesn't like all of us going down there."

"It's safe," said Tia. "Kind of scary, but you can't get hurt if you watch your step."

"I'll l-lead the way!" Rabbit set off with an air tank on his back, holding a torch like a flag. As he pushed aside the leather curtain leading into the long tunnel Tia shivered and wished herself outside in the sunlight.

"This could not have been the original silo entrance," Varas commented on the rough stone walls of the tunnel as they trotted down the steep slope. "Possibly there is an elevator shaft buried somewhere nearby. Your myths mention a Deep Shelter." When they reached the steps he noticed that these too, were of primitive design, built around the inside of the silo as a means of access to the missile, which could never have been originally intended.

"I'm staying up here with Sophia," Ashira said from the gloom behind them. "She needs someone to hold the lights and I can see all I want to from here." To illustrate her point she turned on the photographic lights.

In the pit below them the ancient missile protruded from the earth that had closed around its lower half. It cast a black pointed shadow on the wall behind. Seeing the pit in adequate light for the first time, Tia noted something even more interesting than the rocket. Along the wall behind it was the remnants of a railing and behind the railing, a door.

"Look," she said to Rabbit. "Did you ever see that?"

"No! Th-that m-must be the vault the Major was always talking about."

"Careful," warned Varas. "For all you know that doorway opens onto an elevator shaft."

But it didn't. It led through a short low tunnel into a cavelike space cluttered with piles of old metal and plastic. Against one wall stood an oblong assemblage. Where dials and lights had once gleamed in control panels now empty holes remained. For some odd reason tree branches had been pounded into some of the holes. Rows of antique hubcaps were peg-mounted above the instrument panel like small shields.

"Axles, truck frame—that is a camshaft from an

internal combustion engine. The rest can only be guessed at."

"The Major said the vault was full of treasure," There was contempt in Tia's voice. "Some treasure."

"But more valuable than gems," said Varas. "For this treasure enabled them to live, to make tools and weapons." He picked up an ancient axe head red with rust and weighed it in his hand. "This is probably much too heavy for them now. Sad . . ." He turned to leave and motioned the children to follow. He barely glanced at the missile.

"What did you find?" Ashira wanted to know as they made their way carefully up the steps toward her.

"The origin of some myths," Varas replied. "As usual, they were disappointing." He then switched to advanced imagery far too sophisticated for Tia and Rabbit to follow. They had almost reached the door when the warbler on the fence alarm went off, its whoops echoing and reechoing through the valley.

"Stay in there!" Mark ordered. "They're throwing rocks at us." He couldn't quite believe what he was seeing. "One minute there's nobody here, the next minute there's an armed mob charging us."

"Should I use my stun gun?" asked Deirdre from her spot on the roof.

"Are you in danger?"

"Not so long as we can hide behind the belfry."

"Hold off then."

"They're putting women and children first,"

reported Mark, "and nine very dirty naked males."

"S-s-simples!" said Rabbit and then answered the unspoken question. "Th-they don't have any m-minds. The Fathers m-make them do the real h-heavy work."

Before anyone could stop her, Tia darted past the adults and out to the door to see what was happening. The expedition members had taken refuge in the amphibians. The grass around the cars was littered with rocks and clods of dirt. Rapidly approaching the fence was almost the entire population, those in front being forcibly driven with clubs by the men behind them. They were all doing a lot of angry yelling but it was hard to tell over the warbler's noise if the anger was directed toward the strangers or each other. Well to the rear, completely out of any danger as they would judge it, walked the Fathers. Tia ducked behind the door frame as a rock lobbed past her and clunked against a bench.

"You were just wanting to meet them all," Ashira grinned at Varas. "Here's the ideal opportunity." A clod of grass and earth whished past, disintegrating as it flew, and landed at her feet. There were more rocks and thuds as the amphibians were hit.

Suddenly Tia's fear was gone and in its place came anger. How dare they! In a crouching run she dodged out the door and over to the lead car where half the expedition members had taken refuge.

Mark opened the car door and pulled her inside.

"Shut off the alarm," she told him. "I want to talk to them."

"Use this." He handed her a mike and with his other hand turned on the car speaker. Her appearance had caused a slight lull in the shouting. Then from the rear of the mob a voice yelled and a new volley of stones hit the cars.

"Stop it!" She held the mike too close to her mouth and the words hissed and crackled. "Stop it! Are you all Simple?"

At the taunt the yelling subsided into a muttering wonder at the sound of her voice over the amplifiers. As if intimidated both by the volume and the fact that she spoke to them in their own language, the mob came to a ragged halt.

"Drop the rocks!"

"Kill it!" screamed a Father from somewhere behind one of the larger trees. "Don't listen to it! Kill it!"

Tia remembered that voice. "You're so brave when you have a tree to hide behind. Why don't you come up front, Karl?" She heard the people exclaim at her knowledge of his name. "Karl?" she called again.

From the belfry she received an image of two men with bows and arrows trying to creep close enough to kill somebody. The fear returned.

"Stun them both," came Ashira's command, "then move the car up so we can get in."

There was a sharp pop! pop! One man clutched his arm, the other his chest and then each went limp and dropped.

During the hubbub, Mark eased the car up

directly in front of the open church doors. The car door winged fully up provided a shield against all but the best aimed rocks. It was with relief that Tia gave the microphone to Ashira as the woman slid into the already crowded car.

"Who is your leader?" Ashira's accent was heavy but understandable.

There was no response at first, then a sullen muttering and heads turned to look back at the trees.

"I think it's Father Karl, the Major's oldest son," said Tia.

"Is Karl your leader?"

"I-it's him!" came Rabbit's excited response. "I s-saw a couple p-people nod their heads. He m-must be the new m-m-Major."

"If it is the man named Karl, will he step up now and talk with us? If not, you had better choose a leader for you have none."

In the hush that followed all heads turned to look back to where a man stood hidden behind a large cottonwood tree. Slowly an avenue opened in the crowd as they stepped aside in silent expectation of his coming.

"Why do I have to go?" Tia heard his desperate shout. "No other Major ever had to do this. I don't want to die! It's not fair."

"Karl. You will not die. Get up here!"

Slowly, and obviously much against his natural inclinations, the man stepped out from his hiding place and approached the aliens.

17

"B-boy," said Rabbit. "He-he s-sure got t-taller s-since we left." Ashira found this observation of sufficient interest to share it with the rest of the crew.

"How old is he?" Elaine asked.

"Sixteen or seventeen," said Tia.

He was less than five feet tall and looked twice his age. He wore a greasy leather tunic over a loose leather skirt. On his feet wooden platforms with elevated heels were tied on over leggings. With both hands he clutched a stout club raised and ready to strike. Except for scraggly chin whiskers, his face was beardless and his long oily hair was tied back in a ponytail.

As Karl approached, the Base people backed away. The Simples, seeing how close he was getting, began to jabber and then bolted. Their fear of him clearly was greater than their fear of the newcomers. Karl didn't even glance at them.

"Are they moving out of respect for him?" Varas asked the children. "Is that the custom? To leave a definite amount of space around the leader?"

"No." Both shook their heads. "I think maybe he made a new rule—or they're scared of him," said Tia.

"H-he was always m-mean," Rabbit remembered.

"The m-Major let h-him do anything to anybody."

"And possibly he has since the Major's death," said Ashira. She turned on the mike again. "Why did you order your people to attack us? We had harmed no one."

Karl did not answer. He stared sullenly at the ground.

"He thinks you're going to punish him."

"Why?" asked Ashira. "How do I get through to him? How do we get through to any of them? Karl, what do you think we are?" No response. "We are people—like yourselves," she told him.

To that statement Karl did respond. He said, "Bullshit!"

Tia and Rabbit both blushed, embarrassed to hear this crudity spoken in front of the Morrowans. But the Morrowans were only confused.

"What possible relevance does the excreta of male bovidae have to the current situation?" Varas was puzzled.

"None," said Tia. "Uh, what he said was—well, I guess you might call it a 'verbal bridge.' He means he doesn't believe you, but he doesn't know how to say that."

"Oh?" Varas's brow remained furrowed, then a smile of discovery lit his face. "It was an obscenity! Wasn't it? A vulgarism used in place of thought! I've read about them but it never occurred to me the custom was retained here. Fascinating! Their first word to us is an obscenity."

"Revolting."

Laughter greeted Elaine's predictably outraged response. Then, as the full absurdity of their entire present situation hit them, the Morrowans' chuckles turned into guffaws. The mike was still on and the roar of laughter emitted by the amplifiers filled the commons.

The effect of the sound on the people outside was curious. Their initial reaction was fear at the volume of noise. Then as they recognized that noise as laughter, they began to look at each other in wonder. These creatures are people, their expressions said, but what are they laughing at? And the most obvious answer was . . . Karl.

It was as if they dared to remember now they had never liked him and as the Morrowans' laughter continued, the people outside the fence joined in. The Fathers who were his rivals dared first to laugh. The other men followed and it proved so infectious that soon even the women and girls were laughing. Rather carefully, but laughing.

Karl, not quite sure how he should act, tried glaring them down, but the infection had spread too far for fear of him to stop it. His glare only made them laugh harder.

Tia and Rabbit didn't fully understand what was so funny and sat with half-puzzled smiles. Ashira, too, didn't laugh. She was busily studying the crowd.

"We've accidentally created a tenuous bond," she decided, "and a new problem. The laughter may destroy whatever effectiveness their leader has."

The laughter had lessened some of the fear and hostility. The Base people moved closer now in curiosity. Slowly, cautiously to prevent alarm, the expedition members came out of the amphibians. Perhaps emboldened by the sound of a female voice, several of the older Base women shyly approached the fence.

"Should we turn off the current?" asked Mark.

"Not yet," Ashira decided. "We are not . . ."

"What were you doing in my church?" Karl's voice was full of righteous indignation. He had apparently decided some position had to be taken if only to save his face. "What were you doing in my Church? It is a sacred and holy place. You have no right to go in there."

"Sacred to whom?" asked Varas, when Rabbit translated silently.

"It belongs to the Major. I am the Major. People only can go where I say they can. They can go . . ."

"To whom is this building sacred?" Varas asked again. "Who or what is your god?"

"What I say it is," said Karl. "I am Major now."

"Until your Father comes back," called a man's voice mockingly.

Karl ignored that. "Don't go there again," he told the Morrowans without looking at them. "There's power in my church. It can kill you if I say so. I'll make it kill you if you don't go away!"

"What power is that, Karl?"

"It's a secret—a secret of the Old People."

"We already showed them the Missile," blurted Tia. "They know it's a piece of junk. The only way it's ever going to hurt somebody is if it falls on them. It's true!" She raised her voice so they all could hear. "Your Missile is a piece of junk."

There were angry denials.

"Tia." Ashira was not pleased. "Don't seek personal vengeance. Don't destroy their faith when you have nothing to take its place. Nothing they can understand."

"But it is junk. You know it. We all know it."

"But these people do not. To them the Missile is a god. And whatever law they have, whatever acceptance of their lives, comes from their belief in that power. If you destroy their faith, when you have nothing to give them in its place, you act without ethics. You take all and give nothing. They have a system that enables them to live. We may not approve of that system, but unless we can give them a better one, which they can absorb, don't destroy this one out of anger."

"But they're all slaves to the Fathers because of this."

"Better slavery than starvation. If we cause a revolt, we can leave. They may die."

Tia was chagrined at the reprimand. She did not fully understand Ashira's objection.

Before she could stop and sort it all out something else caught her attention. There was, standing at the rear of the crowd, a scared old woman who was blind in one eye. With her good eye she was staring at Tia and had been since the girl had first emerged from the amphibian. Now she began to sidle her way through the ranks of men in front of her, pushing apologetically like a stray dog expecting a kick. When she reached the clot of women near the front, she put her hand on the shoulder of one. If the old woman was familiar to Tia, the one she now touched was even more so. Behind the grime that covered the younger woman Tia recognized Letty, her mother, and then, with a less painful shock, realized the old woman was the kitchen worker, Anna.

Anna spoke and gestured toward Tia. Letty stood stolidly as if deaf. Anna tugged at the other's arm as if to pull her along. The young woman yanked her arm away. "But it's her!" Anna's voice raised. "Can't you hear? It's her come to life again. Your first child! Look at her. The one who left with the boy. The old Major . . ."

At that the young woman struck the old woman an audible blow on the head. Anna reeled but managed to stay on her feet. She pressed one gnarled brown hand against her head and looked at her attacker with a mixture of pity and contempt. Then that one eye surveyed the rest of her kinsmen. "Why should you know her? You never looked at her when she was with us," she said. "You just used her as the goat. Her and the boy." No one answered and after a moment Anna turned and walked toward the

Morrowans. She passed Karl without a glance. The people of the Base fell silent, waiting to see what would happen to her.

"Turn off the fence." Ashira, cued to Tia, had missed none of the incident. David stepped forward and opened the gate. Without hesitation Anna came into the enclave and the fence was turned on again. She was obviously uneasy, but determined as she walked up to Tia and asked, "It is Tia, isn't it?"

"If you are thinking of embracing her, don't," came Lora's warning. "She's filthy and there's no chance to disinfect."

"It's not allowed here," Tia advised and found that for once the Morrowans were delighted by inhibitions. To Anna she spoke. "Yes, I'm Tia—I told the women that when we stopped in the field."

"I wasn't in the field," Anna said simply. "I was in the kitchen. The other short one, is that the boy, Rabbit? The one you ran away with?"

Tia nodded and Rabbit, used to Morrow's customs, bowed toward the old woman.

"Where did you run to? Where did these people find you? Do you work for them now?"

"A long way from here. We. . . ."

"You always knew they were out there didn't you? That's why you were so different."

"Not always. It's hard to explain, Anna."

The old woman smiled, revealing her one remaining front tooth. "You remember my name! All clean and safe and well and you remembered my name." She was so pleased.

Ashira stepped back to the nearest car and brought out a folding wooden stool. She opened it and placed it beside Anna. "Please sit, Anna," she said slowly, carefully. "The excitement must be tiring for you."

Anna's smile broadened. "Thank you, Father." She picked up the little stool and examined it carefully, folding and unfolding it. "Isn't that pretty!" she said admiringly, then she put it back down and sat on it. "And it works, too! For all it's pretty . . ."

While Tia translated, Anna surveyed the goggled faces around her. "You people don't look . . . well, I shouldn't say that, it might make you mad. What I mean is, I'm afraid of you—even you two. You're not like you were at all. But at least when I'm scared of you, it's interesting. It's something new for me to see before I die. At my age you like that." She leaned toward Tia and said in a lower voice, "Letty knows you, girl. She's just scared."

"If I may ask, how old are you, madam?" Varas asked in basic Base.

"I'm forty-seven, Father, the oldest person here. How old are you?"

"I am sixty-one."

Anna's gums flashed as she gave a snort of laughter. The thought of anyone living to be sixty-one, or wanting to, was the best joke she'd heard in months. Then as she thought of something else her laughter died away. "Tia, what did you and the boy come back for? To get even? The old Major's not here no more. He went off after you two with some of his men. We ain't seen them since, and," she confided in a lower voice, "I think he's dead. Maybe all of them are. Unless he's with you." Alarmed at that thought she half rose from her seat and peered about as if expecting to see the man.

"He is not here," said Ashira before Tia could speak.

"Where is my father?" Karl, feeling left out of things, shouted the question. "Where is my father?"

"He is dead," said Ashira. "He died by the sea."

"The Witch killed him!"

"No. I shot him."

"He d-deserved it, too!" Rabbit stepped forward. "He was tr-trying to kill me with a r-rock." The little boy removed his protective eyeshades, pushed back his hood, and squinted in the sunlight. "In c-case you d-don't recognize m-me, I'm r-r-Rabbit. I used to l-live here. S-so did Tia." He pointed at her. "Anna knows us."

There were mumblings and whisperings among the Base people. They recognized him, or his stutter.

"Does that mean the old Major won't ever come back?" a voice called.

Rabbit frowned. "Ashira just s-said he was dead. D-d-didn't you hear h-her?" He put his shades back on to protect his eyes.

"That a female?" Karl pointed at her.

"Yes," said Rabbit. "S-she's the Elite of Morrow and . . ."

"My father would never let a female kill him. You're all liars! I don't know what else you are, but you're all liars. My father could kill any man here. How do you think he stayed Major?"

"H-he's dead now," Rabbit cut in. "Him and all his m-men. Why do you th-think they n-never came back?"

"Rabbit," Ashira intervened, "it's pointless to prolong a discussion of this type with Karl. Let's talk with some of the others if we can."

18

"It was nice to see Karl scared for a change," Tia said. "He really is a—an unpleasant person, like Varas says."

Although it was just night, both children were in bed in the back of Car No. 2. It had been a long day and they were supposed to be sleeping, but they weren't. The flood lights on the church lit up the tents and the trees cast dark shadows against the surrounding cabins. Behind the red winking fence the Morrowans sat silently, resting, some communicating either with each other or with friends back on the ship. A guard detail had been formed with some awkwardness. There had never been anyone to fear attack from before. Of all the Morrowans, Tia and Rabbit were the only ones who really felt at ease. They trusted the adults to protect them should anything go wrong.

"It's funny, huh?" said Tia.

"Seeing Karl scared?" thought Rabbit.

"No, I wasn't even thinking about that. Seeing this place again—and knowing we don't have to stay here."

"Everything is so dirty. It stinks! I never noticed that when we lived here."

"Me neither. And it's all so small. And dark."

"I guess we're used to bigger rooms now. And windows."

"You know what?"

"What?"

"I wish I could take a bath." He scratched his arm and shifted position. "I didn't shower last night because of the mosquitoes. When I was here I never washed and it didn't bother me. Now I feel uncomfortable when I'm dirty. Maybe our skins are getting soft from wearing clothes?"

There was no answer from Tia and after a minute or so Rabbit sat up on one elbow and whispered, "Are you s-s-sleeping?"

"Thinking."

"What about?"

She shrugged. "I don't know. A lot of things. The look on Ashira's and Varas's faces when they saw where we slept. And how the people here acted when we arrived. I mean, they always thought there was nobody else in the world—but when we showed up, it didn't make them glad, or curious. Just scared. Nobody asked any questions. The only thing they seemed interested to hear was that the old Major was dead—now I suppose the other Fathers will try to club Karl."

"He deserves it!"

"That's not the point. We look better, cleaner, and well fed and dressed. But none of them asked why. Not one person said, 'Where do you come from?' They don't even know the fence will shock them.

They're afraid of the red lights flashing."

"They're kinda dumb, huh?"

"Why do you suppose they got more friendly when they learned the Major was dead? That would scare me. He was the most powerful man they had and the smartest."

"And the meanest." Rabbit changed the subject. "Did your sisters say anything to you?"

"You were with me all the time."

"Yeah. They just looked. None of the boys talked to me either." They withdrew into private thought for a moment, then Rabbit wondered, "What happened to Anna's eye?"

"A hot coal exploded in the fire and hit her face."

He shivered. "That must have hurt!"

The left rear corner of the amphibian creaked as if a spring had coiled and a shudder ran through the metal floor beneath their sleeping bags.

"What was that?"

"It's just squeaking to itself," Rabbit decided with assurance. "All cars do that—especially when they cool off at night. The panels snap sometimes when . . ."

The car creaked again, louder this time. Tia thought she felt it move. "Something's wrong," she said aloud and sat up. As if her sudden movement caused it, the rear end of the big vehicle dropped a few inches. "Ashira!"

"What is it?" And on learning the cause of their worry, "Pat—Henri? Check the hydraulic suspension on No. 2. Tia says the rear end just dropped," and to the children, "It's all right."

Then Tia saw Ashira rise from her place at the table where she had been drinking coffee with Luiz and Saidia. She blanked thought to Tia but couldn't control her expression as quickly. The look of utter dismay communicated better than any thought. And it was not only on Ashira's face but all the faces that turned toward Car No. 2.

"Stay still," came her command, "both of you. Now, if you can do so without shifting, open your sleeping bags. Tell me when they are open."

"What's wrong?" Rabbit wanted to know.

"Open your sleeping bags. Slowly."

Tia saw Mark get into Car No. 3. "Don't watch Mark, Tia. Get out of that bag." Ashira started to walk toward them and Varas grabbed her shoulders almost roughly. "No!" was all he said but the fact that he said it aloud and in that particular tone to Ashira gave Tia a cold chill. All of a sudden she didn't want to even consider what must be wrong but instead obediently reached up and began to lift the velcro grippers apart.

"Mine's open," reported Rabbit, "Why . . ."

"Don't think. Just listen and obey." The car lurched backward with a sickeningly abrupt drop and Tia slid flat on her back and struck her head on the floor which seemed to come up to hit her. Rabbit's knees lodged against her side and she felt his full weight slide against her through the padding of the sleeping bag. The car windows were almost vertical when she looked at them, not horizontal. She could see out but where Car No. 3 should be there was only the stone pile of the church. She twisted her head. Car No. 1 was pulling away. She could see people running.

"Don't leave us! What's happening?"

"Earthquake! Earthquake!"

The shouts came from the darkness of the village behind the trees. The old bell in the church tower clonked erratically as if tapped by ghostly hands. Tia could smell new earth and torn grass. The car slipped again and the caterpillar treads moved. Beneath them something cracked as though the earth had broken one of its bones. They were rolled slowly backward, downward.

"Are you conscious?" Ashira's tone was almost casual. "Tia? Rabbit? Good. Now just stay as you are. Don't try to move. I don't think you can open the doors now." With effort she remained calm. "Mark and Saidia are backing up the other cars to tow you out. Just sit still until I tell you to move."

But neither of them could do that. "We're sinking into the ground," Rabbit thought, wonderingly, and they were. The flood lights showed a distinct depression in the earth, like a green bowl with a ragged rim. One side of it, the side nearest the church, was already deep enough to cast the windows of the amphibian into shadow. The amphibian sat near the middle of the depression, sinking faster into the earth below.

"It's not an earthquake," Varas's analysis seemed as calm as if this were an every day event. "The old missile silo is collapsing from the weight of the cars."

At that Tia felt a sick surge of terror. In her mind that missile silo would always remain as she saw it first when a very small child—a pit deep and dark and filled with horror. The thought of falling into it from the surface and being entombed in the car with tons of earth falling in upon them . . .

For the first time she disobeyed Ashira, threw back the sleeping bag covers still warm from her body, pushed Rabbit away and struggled to sit upright. The amphibian lurched and she grabbed at anything.

"Wh-what are you doing! You're making it s-slide more!"

She didn't answer but grabbed hold of the stretcher track in the floor and pulled herself along. The amphibian was tipped back at a forty-degree angle now and rising. Each move she made seemed to tip it more. But it wasn't actually her struggles that caused the problem but the collapse of the structure below them. She grabbed onto the back of a seat and gained a yard, and using the seats as a ladder, pulled herself to the front of the car and into the driver's seat.

The rear of the car was now in shadow; the front, tilted up into the light from outside. Rabbit, seeing where she had gone, understood immediately what she was trying to do but doubted her ability to do it. "You've never dr-driven a b-big car—and . . ."

The front wheels left the ground and the car jolted down onto its half-tracks and began to roll back. "The brakes! Where's the brake button?" And then Tia saw it before anyone could tell her. Right panel—third button. She hit it with the palm of her hand and for a second thought, "it's not going to hold," for the heavy vehicle continued its frightening downward creep as she looked for the "Power On" switch.

"Put it in l-l-low gear," called Rabbit as he dug himself out of a tangle of sleeping bags and equipment that was beginning to shift to the bottom as the gravity center of the car changed. "Ouch!" Something clonked off his head.

Tia didn't even hear him—or any of the instructions now pouring in from the Morrowans as they saw where she was. She was totally absorbed in survival. She pressed the "Power On" switch and heard the faint whine of the motor waiver as the chassis rocked on its suspension. She remembered the little trucks at Morrow had two gears, and this car had more, and separate drives for the rear wheels or tracks—it didn't matter now. She would go straight ahead and if that didn't work . . .

She put the car into gear and the power full on— and the car didn't move forward. But it did quit creeping backward. Grabbing the steering bar as if she could force the car ahead by sheer will, she rammed her foot against the reserve power switch. Precious seconds passed before she remembered to release the brakes. The car slipped back several swift

yards and she heard a scream. The light disappeared and a wall of earth rose ahead of her.
Then, slowly, the half tracks dug in and now ever so
slowly began to creep forward, walking the car up
out of its trap.

Sounds of creaking were audible all around them
now. It was hard to tell if they came from the earth
or the tortured car. Light touched the nose of the car
like a benediction as it inched up—so slowly up. The
front wheels were in the air again. The amphibian
was standing at a 60° angle as the car approached the
brim of the depression. Rabbit, frozen with fear and
anticipation, lay on his stomach, holding onto a seat
and just watching and waiting. Tia couldn't steer
now; she didn't know how to maneuver the rear
treds, but only force the vehicle up. If it would go up
further.

When the car reached the point where it could tip
over backward with very little encouragement,
Ashira's thoughts for one flash were sheer private
hell. But that instant gave Tia both insight and
determination. "Don't worry," she answered with
intuitive assurance. "We aren't going to die." And as
if in final response to her will, the car tipped forward, then rocked back on its suspension, teetered
sickeningly, slammed its front wheels down on solid
ground and lurched ahead.

The normally quiet Morrowans went wild with
cheering as the big car lumbered out across the
commons.

"Shut off the power! Shut off the power!" Mark

shouted. "You're clear! Shut it off!"

Tia reached up almost automatically and pressed the switch and the car shuddered to a halt short of an old cottonwood. Almost immediately hands were on the doors. The frame was bent. The door on the right side couldn't be opened. But the left door raised.

"Hi," Rabbit said rather weakly from where he lay on his stomach on the floor, chin in hands.

"Are you hurt? Can you move?" Lora's torchlight swept his body and she pushed people back from pulling him out, fearing injury.

"I'm okay." He twisted about and sat up. "Just s-s-shook up. B-b-boy was I s-s-scared! That was really s-s-smart, Tia!" He shook his head in admiration. "Did you s-s-see what s-she did?" he asked the onlookers.

"I couldn't have done it better myself. If I had thought of it in time," Mark said. "She walked it right out of there! Tia, Tia? Are you with us?"

Tia was still sitting in the driver's seat, hands gripping the steering bar, which was trembling in her grip. Her knees were shaking so hard her feet made a scuffing noise against the floorboards as she stared without seeing through the windshield. The adults looked at one another and no one smiled.

But Tia was unaware of both what her body was doing in reaction to prolonged sudden fear, and of the others around her. She had taken momentary refuge in analyzing that one agonized flash from

Ashira. For an instant during the cave-in Ashira's mind had relived another disaster. As she watched this amphibian sink she saw again another car crossing a meadow by a river, a small open car which the earth betrayed.

Without warning an ancient storage tank had totally given way beneath it. The car dropped into a deep pool of viscous black mud. "Drowned in darkness. He loved light and he drowned in obscene darkness." That was the overriding thought Ashira's mind replayed, the thought Tia picked up. Someone else Ashira loved had gone down into blackness with his eyes and mind open, communicating to her. And the grief was fresh after ten years. For that instant tonight, thinking she was going to see it happen again to two more that she loved, she relived the past.

By the degree of the woman's grief, Tia could finally believe there was no pretense—Ashira did love them. As equals. For in some way, they had partially replaced the lost love.

By the time the villagers approached the fence, Tia had dropped her head onto her arms and was shaking with sobs. The shaggy people watched sullenly as Mark reached in and gathered her up and carried her over to where a very quiet Ashira stood waiting. Tia's first coherent thought came when she saw that pale face. "I had to do it," she said. "I knew you'd miss us if we died, too."

19

By the time the two of them settled down to sleep again most of the confusion was over. The flood lights on the church were set to light only the camping area and leave the cave-in in darkness. Wink lights pulsed on what remained of the fence. Car No. 2 was jacked up for damage assessment and repairs were underway.

But no one slept much that night. Tia lay wide-eyed thinking, staring at the tent roof, hearing footsteps in the grass. Rachets clicked and power tools whined from Car No. 2. The coffeepot rasped against the grate as those on guard duty drank to keep alert. Sporadic calls came from the darkness of the village. There, too, the people were on guard—against the aliens and whatever it was that had shaken the earth. Then, rather to Tia's surprise, there was morning light and she realized she had slept. Someone close by was yelling.

Rabbit was up and pulling on his boots. "They just saw the hole, I think," he said, seeing her eyes open. "They sound really mad."

"Or scared," suggested Tia after listening for a moment to the shouts from outside.

"We better go see if anyone needs us."

The shouting died as soon as they emerged from their tent—although it didn't occur to them that it was their appearance that stilled the noise.

A morning mist drifted over the trees; the grass was wet and a strong odor of woodsmoke hung in the air. Seeing the Base at this time of day brought back memories for Tia of being wakened by the cook's shout and crawling from a cold bed to run barefoot and freezing to the latrine. "From there I'd have to run to the kitchen to help him fix breakfast for the women. And wash the slimy wood dishes in cold water and then run out to the field and help my mother—and get yelled at everytime one of them felt like yelling or hitting." She shivered, not from cold.

"Why don't you go back where you come from?"

They looked over at the men standing at the far edge of the fence surrounding the pit. It was impossible to tell who had asked the question. All looked equally angry.

"There's men up in the trees," said Rabbit. "I guess they wanted a better view. Let's go look at the hole."

"I don't see Ashira or Varas."

"They're probably still sleeping. Look where Tom is!" He pointed to the church top where (between two obviously weary guards) the photograper sat, busy with his camera. "Tom doesn't like to miss anything. Come on, let's go look."

"Don't get too close to those people," came a guard's tacit warning. "We don't want an incident."

"Okay, we'll stay by the church."

Parallel lug holes in the ground led to the edge of the cave-in. It was a rough bowl almost fifty feet across and as deep. Further sinking in the night had erased the tracks of the amphibian except where a few feet of undisturbed sod remained in the near center. A deep trench led halfway back toward the church.

"It's hard to believe we got out of there."

"But we did. We're pretty smart!"

Tia grinned down at him. "Pretty lucky, too," she said.

One of the men in the trees shouted. "You know what the hole is?" he yelled excitedly, "It's above where the Missile stands! It's above the Sacred Vault! See? There, part of the tunnel sank in. They buried the Missile!"

"No!" That was Karl's shout. "The Missile would explode if anything touched it."

"Get your butt up here and see for yourself, Karl. If you figure which direction you turn when you go down the tunnel . . ."

They began to argue. Several ran off toward the Fathers' house. Others inched closer to the fence.

"I think we better wake Ashira and Varas," Tia decided.

"I want to get into my church," Karl shouted. "You, witch, tell your people to get out of the way."

"You c-can't go down there, Karl," Rabbit told him. "It's all caved in."

"Who says so?"

"Our people," said Tia. "They checked last night. The tunnel collapsed about twenty feet from the entrance."

"You're lying, witch!"

"Sh-she's not either! The hole is filled up. And it's a g-good thing. I always hated that Missile. And so does everybody else!"

Karl glared at them, his mouth half open. Then he looked more closely at the pit. "You did it! You came back here on purpose . . . and you probably did kill Otto like my father said. We should have killed you both when we had the chance. Bashed your heads . . ." He was about to work himself into a rage but he stopped abruptly, as if deciding that if they could kill Otto without touching him and bury the Missile without harm to themselves, then they were truly to be feared. He wheeled around and, seeing men running off to alert the other Fathers, he ordered, "Get back here! Now!" Rather unwillingly, the men did as he ordered. They huddled together to talk, as if fearing Tia and Rabbit would overhear, and then with many backward glances all slowly left.

"What do you think he's going to do?" Rabbit wondered.

"Try to figure out some way to keep people from learning the Missile is dead."

"Why? It doesn't change anything."

"Yes, it does," said Tia. "Now a Major doesn't have anything to scare people with. That's why they obey the Majors—they've always been scared not to."

Ashira decided after being appraised of the situation, "Put the fence around our camp. Let them back into the church. Varas and I will make our apologies for the damage. We'll spend the rest of the day compiling information and collecting specimens. If possible, Lora and Don want to treat a few patients. If the repairs on the car are complete, we should leave tomorrow. I see little point in prolonging our visit."

As the Morrowan delegation walked from their enclave to the Fathers' mess hall, several of the Base hunters and soldiers approached them in a challenging manner and then drew back, afraid. And in truth there was something vaguely threatening about the Morrowans' appearance.

The hooded androgynous dress, combined with the deeply tinted eyeshades that concealed the upper portion of their faces, gave them a totally impersonal air. The fact that sunlight reflected off the suits in subtle dazzle, and the eyeshades mirrored images, added to their inhuman aura. As they entered the mess hall, David went in first, gun in hand; Deirdre remained behind in the doorway, her collecting stun gun loosely cradled in her right arm.

The Fathers, threatened by the very appearance of strangers in their village, and made more nervous by the huge pit on the commons, panicked when the visitors boldly walked in. Benches were kicked over, tables pushed sideways, wooden dishes clanked to the floor and bounced as the men jumped to their feet and knocked each other down in their panic to get away.

Tia and Rabbit smiled. The sight was very satisfying to them.

"Don't run!" Tia yelled over the confusion. "Sit down! Don't run. Karl! Tell them to stop before someone gets hurt." She didn't mean it as a threat, but it was understood that way. Karl's face went pasty with fear. Several of the other men looked as if they were going to be sick. A semblance of quiet fell.

"We come to apologize for the damage to the old silo," Ashira began.

"What silo?" asked a sullen voice. "The only silo we got is down by the cow barn with corn fodder in it. You wreck that, too?"

"We refer to the old Missile silo . . ." Ashira surveyed their blank hostile faces. "The weight of one of our cars caused the top of the cave to collapse. As apparently some of your people have guessed, the Missile is now completely buried—as well as most of the tunnel leading to it."

"You're lying! It would have exploded . . ."

"No . . ."

"It would have!" Karl ignored Varas's interruption. "I could make it explode by touching it! Everybody here knows that. My father told me so. And the Major before him knew it . . ."

"How tiresome," Ashira thought as she waited for the desperate tirade to end. "Does he—do they all believe this, Tia?"

Tia shrugged. "They did. But after they all see that hole, I don't think they will. No matter how hard Karl tries to tell them otherwise. I don't think he'll be strong enough to punish everyone who doubts him anymore."

Ashira nodded and gave a surprisingly shrill whistle that stopped Karl in mid-mouth. "If you truly have faith, then the Missile still lives. It's buried now—but no less powerful than it ever was."

Ignoring Ashira, Karl glared at Tia. "It's your fault. You did it! I saw you in that thing pushing the ground in. You and this stuttering Simple. I'll get you for this!" He took a step toward her, fist raised, menacing.

"Enough!" Varas stepped forward and Karl paused. "They were merely driving the car out of the hole. There is nothing to blame them for. You are a stupid man—something your father was not—and unfit to lead your people."

Ashira looked at Varas in astonishment. He was furious. In all the years she had known him, she had never seen him get truly angry.

"It's time to end this interview," she suggested to him, and to the Fathers she said, "We deeply regret destroying both your property and routine. Your church is now open to you but the tunnel is unstable—dangerous to enter. We suggest you do not try to repair it or the silo. We apologize also for interrupting your breakfast."

At the doorway she turned, "We shall be leaving tomorrow. We will try not to further disrupt you in the time we remain here."

The Morrowans were eating breakfast when the women came out of the mess hall to go to work. They stopped at the tool shed where a man issued implements they would need for that day. As they stood in line for the tools, they stared across the commons at the visitors. Tia turned her camp stool so her back was to them.

Tom didn't miss a shot.

Four yoked Simples were led from the cow barn by whip-armed overseers. A big chain rattled over the ground behind them as they were driven off after the women.

"They're probably going to drag in logs," Rabbit explained. "Little logs. For the big ones they use all nine Simples."

Anna came out of the kitchen several times lugging wooden slop pails of dirty washwater which she tipped over a few feet from the kitchen door. The second trip out she waved to the Morrowans. They waved back and she smiled a toothless smile.

"Could we take her back with us?" Tia asked impulsively. "She's the only kind person here . . . Maybe it was a dumb idea?" She let the question hang in air.

"She certainly needs medical attention we can't

give her here," said Lora. "She still has sight in that eye, you know. Scar tissue in the lid keeps her from opening it. If we scrubbed her up and put her in clean clothes, I'd have no objection to riding with her."

"Has she asked to go with us?" Ashira asked Tia.

"No, but she'd want to. Who wouldn't want to get away from here?"

Rabbit nodded agreement with that, as did several Morrowans.

"She would be away from everything she's ever known, a Simple Talker among telepaths. She would be very lonely."

"You're saying no?"

"I'm saying we might not be doing her a kindness, Tia. You discuss it with her. But remember, she would be going into exile."

"But I can ask her?" Tia's face lit up. "She was always good to me."

"Who—what are the men doing?" Rabbit stood up to see better and he was frowning. The Fathers and lesser caste men were all gathering at the tool shed. Some had started walking across the fields in the direction the women had taken.

"They appear to be going to work."

"They never work in the fields or woods," said Tia.

"Maybe Karl has changed some customs?"

"He hasn't changed one custom," observed Tia. "He isn't going to work with them."

Some time later Karl and his henchmen circled the far side of the open pit and entered the church. One of them was carrying a blazing torch. After twenty minutes or so they emerged and went back to their mess hall saying nothing to the workers. The church doors were closed and four soldiers armed with clubs were left on guard in front of them.

Work resumed on the repairs to the car. Luiz and Deirdre set off together to collect specimens about the village. Elaine sat in a car, her eye pressed to a microscope, taping her notes and observations. The children took Varas, Lora, and Ashira to see the school, the smokehouse, and storage cellars.

"From the number of fallout shelters and their size, this was quite a base at one time," Lora remarked. "I wonder what the purpose was. And where the other silos are. And were the personnel stationed here unique?"

"Do you mean was it intended as a refuge for government hierarchy in case of attack? A small LIFESPAN? You think that would explain their survival?" said Ashira.

Lora shrugged. "What do you think, Varas—what will become of these people if we simply go away and leave them to themselves?"

"They'll probably remain static, as they appear to have for generations. As Tia pointed out, they have little to work with. They lack all energy resources but human labor. And sparse oxygen at this altitude hinders that. Even their cattle are too small to pull a plow in tandem. Yet they manage to survive, if not with much grace."

"Do you see them as any great threat to the Balance?" Lora asked Ashira.

"Not if we mind our own business. We can't change anything without changing all. To do that we would have to cross-breed effectively at Morrow— the infants wouldn't survive here. Four generations or more . . ."

Tia shut them out. Sometimes people could be very boring, even smart people, when they thought about things you weren't that interested in. When they got back to camp, Tia and Rabbit took a long nap to make up for the sleep they'd lost the night before. The adults went on speculating.

Instead of sitting on her bench by the back door to the kitchen as she normally did each evening when work was done, Anna came over to the fence and stood watching the visitors pack their cars.

"You're going away again?" she called to Tia as the girl emerged from the rear of the amphibian. Car No. 2 was temporarily repaired, but the mechanics advised putting as little weight into it as possible. This necessitated a lot of repacking into the nearly full remaining two cars. Tia and Rabbit, by virtue of their size, were very good at stowing things into tight corners.

"We're leaving in the morning," Tia called back. "Wait a minute, I'll let you in. I want to talk to you."

"I don't think I should." Anna looked back into the shadows of the village. "They don't like my being friendly." But when Tia opened the gate, Anna came shyly into the compound.

"I guess I won't be seeing you two again. I know how the rest of 'em feel, but I like having you here." She sat down on the stool Tia brought her. "Makes me feel good to see you all shining when you walk about."

"Anna—would you like to go back with us?"

Anna gave her a sharp sideways glance from her

[143]

good eye, then a smile broke over her face. "You're just teasing me," she said.

"No, I mean it. You can come with us! Ashira said it's okay. The doctor, the woman who looked at your face—she said she could fix your eye so you could use it again. And you'd have a little house of your own. Morrow is very pretty. It's much warmer than here and . . ."

Anna held up her hands to stop the flow of words. "Wait. Wait. Let me think." And she did just that for a good five minutes while Tia stood before her, shifting from one foot to another, then finally sat down on the grass. "Do you think they'd let me go?" Anna said finally, jerking her head in the direction of the Fathers' house.

"They wouldn't have to know about it until you got into the car."

"But I'd want to say good-bye to—to a lot of people. I couldn't just up and leave. Who would do my work?"

Tia was about to say, "Anybody can do that work," when kindness stopped her. Anna's work was the only thing the woman had to be proud of; her kindness was considered a weakness here, not a virtue. "Let them worry about that," Tia said instead. "Maybe that will make them appreciate how hard you work."

"I dunno," Anna sighed. "When I was young like you I used to dream about running away and living by myself in the hills. But how would I have lived?"

"Now's your chance—come with us!" urged Tia. "We'll be good to you."

"Yes, you would, I bet. Just like I am to the cows. No—let me say it, girl. I know you mean well. But I know, too, that you're all much smarter than me. I'd be like a dumb animal that needed watching. I wouldn't like that."

"You're afraid," Tia cut in. "You're afraid to go, Anna, that's why you're thinking up all these excuses."

Anna nodded agreement. "Partly, I'm afraid." She put her hand over her heart. "Just thinking about getting into one of those things . . . but the other is true, too. You and your new people are too far above me. I'd be less there than I am here." She saw the disappointment on Tia's face. "But you let me think about it tonight and I'll tell you in the morning. Now I'll just sit here and watch you while you work."

She stayed until long after dark and the lights came on, smiling, watching, drinking the sweet coconut drink Ivan brought her. But unlike the night before, no one else came near the camp. The only sound from the settlement was that of the frogs and night insects.

Anna did not return in the morning. Nor did any one else. The Base appeared as deserted as it was the afternoon they arrived. There were no good-byes. The cars made a U-turn around the church and rolled off past the barns and out between the strawstacks. There were no women working in the fields even though it was long past sun-up.

There were just the four of them in Car No. 2 now. Tom and Lora rode in Car No. 1. The steering on Car No. 2 wasn't responding as it should and Ashira was preoccupied with driving and wondering if the car was going to make it all the way back to the coast. Pat and Henri had test-driven it in the creek and pronounced it fixed and watertight, but Ashira no longer trusted it. She listened to every creak and rattle and expected it to break down any moment.

Varas was preoccupied with something and Tia and Rabbit used telepathy between themselves to avoid disturbing the other two. Not that they had much to say either. The whole visit had been disappointing to the Morrowans. Even though Tia and Rabbit had told them what to expect, they had somehow expected more. As if they could not believe, before seeing the reality, that the only other human survivors in their world were not quite within their concept of "human." And it made them more aware of their uniqueness. More lonely.

"Maybe the car just needed shaking down," Ashira noted. "It seems to be riding more smoothly now."

"They moved the boulders and logs out of the way for us," Mark answered from the lead car. "See the brush piles? They wanted to make it easy for us to leave. You can see the sledge marks where they dragged . . . that's odd. The creek has risen a good two feet."

The lead car dipped and lurched its way between the trees and down the creek embankment into the water. Ashira slowed and swung out to avoid crunching the bottom of her injured car over a huge boulder.

"Stop! We've got troubles," came Mark's call. "Put your cars in reverse and get out of these trees."

"What is it?"

"I don't see them but I think we're about to be ambushed by the natives." He sounded half amused.

Ahead of them where the creek turned to cut between outthrusting rock ledges, a crude but effective dam of stumps and stone had been built across the width of the stream. The lead car was now in the nasty position of having to back up in a narrow space in water too shallow to float it but deep enough to lessen its maneuverability as a land vehicle.

Mark tried to back straight up the way he'd come

down, but the car didn't want to go that way. He pulled forward and backed up the stream bed, then lumbered up the bank nose first.

Tia was engrossed in Mark's struggle and just as his car bounced over the bank and headed toward them, Rabbit yelled, "Look! Behind the last car!"

Tia's head whipped around. Out from seemingly nowhere came a horde of women and girls. Saidia braked to avoid running them down. And as she stopped, from hiding places behind brushpiles and trees, men appeared and hurriedly lugged stumps and rocks to block the way, then all fanned out around the cars but kept at a respectful distance.

"Stay in the cars," warned Ashira. "Nothing they can lift is heavy enough to break the windows."

The other two cars pulled up until they were bumper to bumper with Car No. 2.

"Why are they stopping us?" Rabbit wondered. And the rest of the Morrowans echoed his thought.

"They've gone to a lot of effort for this," Ashira said. "Saidia, if we can frighten them away from behind you, can you back over that debris?"

"Probably, but it might ruin the screws."

"How about that dam?"

"One of us has to check it out first," answered Mark. "If we ram it and it doesn't go down, we might wreck the car. Of course we can blow it up in two minutes, but we've got to get out to set the charge."

"Okay. We're boxed in. Let's find out what they want." She handed Tia the mike. "Ask them?" and flicked on the speaker.

"What do you want?"

At the sound those outside ducked as if threatened. Tia saw some of them dodge behind the nearest tree and wondered what they were afraid of. They'd heard this noise before and it hadn't hurt them. "Why are you doing this? What do you want?" There was a shade of irritation in her voice. "We're leaving. Get that stuff out of our way."

There was no response.

"I don't understand," said Varas. "Is this an attack—or did they go to all this effort merely to prove they were capable of inconveniencing us?"

"You mean, make us feel silly?" asked Rabbit.

"Partially."

"Karl might. He's not too bright."

"Crack!" A rock hit the windshield and ricocheted off.

"Up here!" Karl's shout came from above them and off to the right. After a moment they spotted him up on a rock ledge among the trees. "Now you can look up to me." And when there was no reply, "You might as well get out of those things," he shouted, thinking the reason they didn't answer was because they were deaf. "You're all staying until I get what I want. You're gonna pay for what you did to my Missile."

Tia translated.

"Fascinating," murmured Varas. "Three days of observing us and he still has no conception of his comparative vulnerability."

"But we didn't hurt anybody while we were here.

We just stunned them." Tia explained. "To him and the other Fathers that means you can't hurt them."

"Or we would have?"

Tia nodded.

"Bother!"

"Send out the old Major's brats. They're gonna pay for what they did! They're mine! If he's dead I get what was his—he told me so. Everybody here knows it. Then throw out your axes and your cold fires for night and all your food."

"He wants us—Rabbit and me!"

"To pay for the silo cave-in?"

"To kill us, I think."

"Ridiculous."

"If they don't come out, old Anna's really going to miss you." He gestured and two men came up the slope behind him dragging Anna. "Anna and me had a long talk last night after her visit. She's sorry she can't go with you."

It was hard to tell at this distance, but it seemed to Tia that Anna's face was swollen and bruised. Rabbit's sharp eyes confirmed Tia's suspicions. "They've b-beaten her up!" he said.

There was an almost visible flash of dismay from the cars' occupants at this. Morrowans could be ruthless but deliberate cruelty was beneath them.

"Stay in the cars!" It was a command, not a warning.

"What are we going to do?" Tia wanted to know.

"Consider the situation from all aspects."

Tia looked from Varas's mind to Ashira's. While it

was clear both were upset by the sight of Anna, they were disturbed in a very different way than Tia was. Their reaction was more regret that one mind could treat another badly, and mild "irritation"—that was the only word for it—that they would now be forced to take action. Ashira's prime impulse was to simply eradicate the source of the stress. That would solve Morrow's problem. But ethically she could not do that. She wasn't sure of the long term effect it would have on the Base.

"Th-they're going to h-h-hang her!"

And they were. They had retreated further up the slope to where a tall pine stood. From where he sat on a branch above Anna, a man dropped a rope of plaited vines. At the end of the rope was a slip-loop which Karl caught and put over her head.

Tia was out the door before they could stop her. Both Ashira and Varas made a grab for Rabbit but he twisted free and tumbled out on the ground after her. Just before the car door dropped shut above him, he reached in and grabbed a gun from beneath the seat.

There was a great outcry at the sight of them in the open. As if they took the children's appearance as a sign of surrender by the aliens, the villagers forgot their fears and swarmed toward the narrow clearing, shouting and brandishing their clubs.

The warbler began to whoop but this time the noise had little effect. The villagers had learned it couldn't hurt them.

Tia ducked behind the nearest tree and Rabbit

crouched behind her. The cars behind gave them a solid protective wall. "Let Anna go!" yelled Tia but she couldn't be heard over the noise.

"I'll shoot Karl," Rabbit thought.

"You might hit Anna!"

"I'll get him. You watch the sides." He inched around the tree. "Boy this gun has a fat barrel," he noted as he rested it on a rock ahead of him, took aim and fired. The gun jerked up in his hands.

Being unfamiliar with weapons neither of them had noticed that the gun he'd grabbed was the amphibian's emergency flare gun. An arc of brilliant green flame shot through the trees to the accompaniment of frightened yells. Base men dropped to the ground out of its path. The charge landed, hitting no one but setting some leaves on fire before it sputtered out.

"Come on!" Tia dodged and raced among the trees and Rabbit scrambled after her. Smoke began to rise from the underbrush on the ledge ahead.

Although Tia and Rabbit were now oblivious to everything but their objective, they had spurred the Morrowans from thought to action. In the first rush of villagers after the children, men had attacked the amphibians seeking to knock in the windows with clubs. Windows inched down and stun guns dropped the attackers. From Car No. 1, Pat and Henri slipped out and raced for the dam carrying the demolition gear. Deirdre got out and crouched behind the car with her collecting stun gun and dropped anyone who even looked as though they were going to chase the two mechanics. Mark moved back to guard Car No. 2.

In the melee no one paid any attention to the village women. A group of them hurried through the underbrush after Tia and Rabbit. With them came the older girls. In all their lives they had never had a chance to vent their slaves' anger without suffering severe punishment. Now they had both the chance and the excuse. If she were lucky, Letty could make up for the problem she had caused the Base by having such an unsatisfactory child. The woman, who as a girl had been the old Major's favorite, would feel "special" again.

The children were some twenty yards up the slope.
Their light blue suits could be seen as they dodged
from tree to tree through the smoke. Rabbit had
fired a second flare and the results were even more
satisfactory than the first. He had hit another
brushpile, ignited damp leaves and sent smoke
rolling down the hill, driving the men out of hiding places choking and coughing. He was pleased
with himself.

There was shouting between the whoops of the
warbler, but it was mostly unintelligible. But Tia did
hear one Father yell, "Let the women get the brats.
We gotta put out those fires," and answering shouts
of agreement.

Karl had lost all control of the fracas. He stood up
on the ledge above them with three of his lieutenants
and Anna. The rope lay on the ground; the man in
the tree was gone. There was a puzzled look on
Karl's broad flat face, as if he didn't quite understand how he had so quickly changed from com-
mander to spectator. It was the sudden fear which
contorted his face that made Tia glance in the same
direction he was watching.

"Rabbit! To the right—behind us!"

His head jerked around.

The women swarmed up the slope, their dress and coloring good camouflage among the sunshine and shade. Letty was their leader. In her right hand she grasped a small short-handled, wicked-looking mattock. She was hurrying, as if determined to get something over with. Some of the older girls were at her heels but were careful not to outpace her.

At Rabbit's elbow stood a scrub pine. He rested the gun barrel on one of its branches, and shot a flare right over the women's heads. There were a few startled yells, but nobody ran. They ducked and kept on coming. He fired again, lower.

"I don't want to burn them!"

"Come on!" They took off, frightened, running blindly, up the stone outcroppings of the ledge on which Karl stood. The women came right behind, running faster now, like a pack of hounds that has sighted its prey and moves in for the kill. They had become a mob.

"Catch them!" Karl ordered his trio. The men looked from their leader to the children to the fast-closing pursuers. And then Karl was left alone with his hostage as his men scrambled over the spine of the ledge and fled up the hill to safety. He glanced from them to the armed women, hesitated for a few seconds and then spurted after his men. Anna stood alone.

"Run to the cars," Tia was puffing from excitement and exertion. "Run—we're coming." But Anna stood as if deaf or dazed. "Come!" Tia reached the old woman, grabbed her by the arm and pulled. "Come on. They'll catch us."

"I don't care," Anna said calmly as if there were all the time in the world. "I don't care what you do to me, Karl. I got nothing. I never had more. You can only kill me once."

The warbler stopped and there was quiet. Tia knew she shouldn't be blanking out the Morrowans' attempts to locate them telepathically in the smoky woods—but if she acknowledged Ashira, she'd have to obey. So she didn't. "It's us, Anna. Rabbit and me. Come on! We have to get back to the car! Please!" She tugged on Anna's arm.

Vital seconds passed as this seeped into Anna's understanding. Then she tried to open her eye. "Tia? You still here? Karl caught you?"

"No, but we gotta run! Come on!"

"Let's pull her." Rabbit grabbed Anna's other arm and she moaned.

"Don't! My arm's broke."

Tia's stomach did a sick flip as she saw an ugly purple swelling halfway up Anna's arm. In spite of herself she wished for Ashira.

"Tia!" The woman was angry with worry. Once that anger would have frightened Tia—now it reassured her. "Where are you two? We can't see you for smoke. We're going to blow the dam. Where are you?"

"Up here . . ."

"Letty? You gone crazy?" Anna abruptly roused

herself from her stupor and pushed Tia behind her
to confront the woman with the mattock. The girls
surged around their leader to shove Anna out of the
way with such force that the old woman stumbled,
lost her precarious balance and tumbled over the
ledge to fall to the ground below.

"Anna!"

The girls closed in around Tia and Rabbit; brown
hands reached out to clutch and hold. But they
couldn't quite bring themselves to touch them. They
looked too frightening, too alien, and there were the
myths that had risen about them since they fled.

"Bring her here! I'll get the witch! I'll kill her!"

Tia heard but the words didn't really sink in until
long after. At the moment all she could think of was
that for twelve years she had been the scapegoat of
these girls. She twisted away from them, ducked one
swinging club and felt another graze her back,
kicked one girl down and struck another in the face
with her fist, fighting to get away to the edge—and
trying to see where Anna and Rabbit were. She
heard Rabbit's yell as he half jumped, half slipped
from the rock, and at the same time she was shoved
toward Letty with such force that she fell against the
maddened woman.

Letty had seen her coming and raised the mattock
to strike. Tia's weight caught her off balance. She
tripped backward and sat down hard upon the rock,
the weapon flying back to glance off one of the
people behind her and evoke a wounded scream.

Tia rolled free and from a squat jumped after Rabbit. She landed badly, on one knee and both hands, but scrambled erect.

Rabbit was kneeling beside Anna's crumpled body. "I think she's dead," he told her silently.

A rippling series of small explosions came from the creek. Pieces of wood and rock fragments sailed up above the trees and then rained down. Shock waves quaked the leaves and the ground trembled.

"Earthquake!" a man's voice yelled. "Earthquake!" There were alarmed cries and shouts, sounds of running.

"They blew up the dam," Tia answered Rabbit's questioning look as she knelt beside Anna and shook the woman's still shoulder. Anna made no sound.

"She's dead," Rabbit repeated.

A shot rang out. Someone else fell from the ledge behind them and hit the ground with a thud. Tia glanced over her shoulder. It was Letty.

"The explosion scared off the others," Ashira explained "but not that one. She was going to jump on you. Now get back here while we can still see you."

Tia nodded as if Ashira was there beside her, then reached out and touched Anna's still warm chin. "I'm sorry," she said aloud. "I'm sorry you had to live this way. You were a good person, Anna."

"Dirty brat," Letty was muttering, "Nothing but trouble. Spoiled everything." She groaned and plucked clumsily at the tiny dart in her side. A trickle of saliva ran down her chin. Tia looked from the dead woman to her mother's drugged and twisted face. She began to shake with anger, "I wish you were . . ."

"Don't say that," said Rabbit. "It's hard to live here. She doesn't know any better."

"It was just as hard for Anna," Tia said bitterly. "It's not what she knows. It's what she is—mean!"

A sudden gust of wind blew smoke around them. Tia raised her head to see where the girls on the ledge were. Ashira was right. They had gone and the underbrush where they had been was afire.

"Wow!" breathed Rabbit, following her glance. "I never thought of *that*. We'd better get out of here."

Startled, Tia stood up quickly and nearly fell. She had twisted an ankle in the jump off the ledge. Tiny flames flickered up a dead tree above them and the dry bark crackled and curled off in fragments which drifted, still burning, to the leaves on the forest floor below.

"We can't leave them here." She pointed to the two women. "They'll get burned." She turned to look down at the cars but smoke obscured the view. She knelt and reached out to pull Anna by the arms, then hesitated. Anna was dead. Nothing could hurt her now. Painfully she stood up and hobbled the few steps to Letty's side and forced herself to take hold of one limply outflung arm of the still muttering woman.

Rabbit hesitated, then grabbed Letty's other wrist and together he and Tia tugged her down the slope, with her heels tracing furrows in the leaves and pine needles. She wasn't heavy but she was dead weight and just about as much as they could manage.

"Tia? Rabbit?" Ashira's worry nagged them.

"We're coming." Both of them were coughing from the smoke, their eyes tearing so much they couldn't see where they were going. The brushfire was beginning to generate its own draft and odd little winds sprang up.

They had paused to get their breath. When the flare gun first set the underbrush afire, Tia had thought it a lucky accident that drove off their attackers. But the speed with which the little flames licked up the leaves and grew into bigger flames was scary. She could hear the blaze now, rushing and crackling to itself, and beyond the ledge somewhere the Base men, their shovels and picks striking stones as they tried to contain the various fires.

Rabbit was looking down the slope to see how close the cars were and wondering if perhaps they couldn't just leave Letty here and run for help. The Morrowans were using the loudspeaker, trying to guide them through the smoke. "We're coming," he assured them. "We're okay. I think."

A sudden downdraft cleared the smoke to the east of the woods and Tia saw that the fire had crept across the space between trees and field. A smoldering grassfire was working its way down the corn rows toward the barns. It struck her for the first time that the entire Base might burn. For if those straw and hay stacks caught, the barns would surely go—and then the sheds. In her imagination she could see the village burning, the fire taking away forever all she had once hated and had to endure.

She could see it so clearly, the smoking ruins of the Fathers' House, the mess hall, the girls' dormitory where she had slept. The charred wood would be velvet black trimmed with gray ashes. And then soon the rain would wash away the ash and grass would grow and cover it all. And when people asked to be shown the Base, she could say, "Here's where it was—but it's not there anymore—there is only grass in that upland valley now."

"Tia? Tia?" Rabbit intruded on her fantasy. "Why are you smiling like that?"

For an answer he got a self-conscious grin but no sharing of her thoughts. Instead she started to tug Letty again.

"Let's leave her and run for it. Dr. Lora can get her with the stretcher," he suggested.

"No!" Tia was not sure why she was opposed to that idea, or why she suddenly felt so guilty. "It would take too long getting the stretcher out. They might not find her in the smoke and then they'd be in danger too." Her foot hit a stone at an off-angle and her sprained ankle protested with pain.

But Rabbit's question had reminded her of something she had forgotten. If the village did burn, what would happen to the people? They wouldn't neatly disappear into the purity of fire. The babies in the Infant House might burn. She couldn't count on anyone to risk their life to save them. And others might be injured—but they wouldn't die. Not right away. But what would they all do with no food and no place to sleep? When she and Rabbit reached the cars, Lora would tape her ankle and remove the pain. But if the Base people were hurt, they would either suffer through it or die for lack of medical care.

"Come on. We can go faster." She suddenly urged Rabbit. "The fire's heading toward the barns. Maybe we can stop it."

Rabbit tried to see the fire but the smoke was too thick again and he was too short to see much anyhow. "Okay." He took her word for it. "I don't see how. Hey, watch it! Old Letty's snagged on the underbrush."

A figure loomed out of the haze and for a moment both children nearly panicked, then they saw it wore an inhalator. "I found them!" The convergence call advised those in the cars. Other Morrowans appeared. The now fully unconscious Letty was picked up like a sack of grain and carried away through the pall.

"Anybody else up there?" Malcolm asked as he hurried them through the smoke to where the amphibians waited.

"Anna. Dead. Ashira—Varas?" and Tia told them of the threat to the village. "It's our fault the fires got started. Rabbit's and mine. But if we can plow up the field with the half-track lugs maybe we can stop the grass fire before it gets to the barns."

"And maybe we can't and we'll be encircled by it," said Ashira. She and Varas had remained within the protection of the amphibian. Mark, standing armed guard beside the car, swung the door up and helped Tia and Rabbit in.

"We can go back to the field and see," Tia pleaded even though she thought she understood Ashira's view. The Elite would see no point in further risking Morrowan lives. Ashira seemed to confirm this.

"Why?" she asked Tia. "Why do you care? You of all people? You suffered twelve years with them. And in the end, they would have killed you had we not intervened. And now here they would like to kill us all. Without compunction. Because we have no human reality for them. We are like a natural disaster. You did not deliberately set the fires. But they have served our purpose. They drove the attackers away."

"But their houses will burn!"

"Would you really regret it if the entire Base burned?" Ashira was asking for total honesty. Her mind searched Tia's emotional and confused thoughts until she found the answer she could not easily dismiss, and it pleased her.

"If we let them suffer like that then we are more frightening than the worst of the Simples. Because we *know* better."

Briefly, Ashira shut her out. Just how did one make clear to someone Tia's age the degree of pure and awesome simplicity her mind would reach after intricate progressions and variations? But now it was enough to know that she had an innate sense of ethics that enabled her to put aside desire for personal revenge and see the picture whole. And that's what Ashira wanted most of all to know about this mind—its degree of Balance. She consulted briefly, privately, with Varas, then switched to convergence to explain the situation to everyone else.

Mark considered only the logistics. "There's no room to turn your cars around. We'll have to clear the debris from behind Car No. 3 and then back up into the fields. If we go as a unit, crossing and recrossing the area—perhaps it might work. Depending on how fast the fire is spreading."

"I can go look," Rabbit volunteered.

"You can help move the debris," Ashira said and Rabbit grinned and went with Mark. "Lora, when you're through with that patient, Tia's ankle needs attention. You stay in the car with us, Tia."

Lora and Don had revived the drugged Letty, but not before Elaine took blood and tissue samples. The woman regained awareness with a start and when she saw them bending over her, cried out and would have bolted had they not restrained her until they were sure she was fully awake. Tia watched Don try to help Letty to her feet and offer her a container of fruit juice. She twisted away from his hands, and ran into the woods like a sullen frightened animal. Tia gave an unconscious sigh as she watched her go.

Ashira missed none of this. "I'm sorry," she said, speaking deliberately to hide her total feelings.

"Don't be. You had to stun her."

"No, I'm sorry she is so much less than you want her to be," Ashira explained. And the answer she got surprised her.

"No," said Tia. "I think she is what I truly want her to be. If she, if any of them, were anything more, then I couldn't leave again."

By the time Tia's ankle was taped the route had been cleared behind Car No. 3. Then it seemed to her that it took forever until the last of the expedition members got back into the cars and they could begin moving slowly backward, toward the field.

It was hard to tell where they were in the smoke. Tree trunks would loom up beside the windows; branches whipped the roof panels. With the half-tracks, the cars were awkward to handle in reverse. Ashira steered by the glow of Car No. 3's fog lights in the haze behind her. Mark followed her. When Saidia stopped to make sure she was still on the track, the other two cars had to stop also. It was a long, halting, quarter mile.

Through the windshield, Tia made anxious note that the smoke was clearing over the creek. If she hadn't told them about the grassfire, they would be on their way toward that blue sky, back to the coast, instead of heading into a place that made the dashboard warning lights flash danger as the scent of smoke seeped through the air filters. The knot of nerves was back in her stomach.

"No. 3 car is in the field and clear," Saidia announced. "We can see your lights, No. 2. You'll clear in ten yards. We will advise when to turn."

Several minutes more and all three big cars were

in formation and ready to begin their march across the stubble field to create the firebreak. They considered lighting a backfire and decided against it. It would involve getting out of the cars to do it, and the gesture might be misinterpreted and provoke hostile reactions.

As the amphibians emerged into less dense smoke, ahead and to the left a band of Base men was working frantically to stop the grassfire. They were naked, using their leather garments as sacks to beat the flames. Sparks and sooty ash flew about them, falling onto bare skin and shaggy hair, causing them to slap themselves and each other. Tia saw some of them walking barefoot on smoking ground and she winced in involuntary sympathy.

When they saw the cars some fled but most kept on working. There was no time to worry. Fire was the older, more feared enemy. Most of the people who had followed Letty were now using their tools to rip up sod in the next field. The grass was long there, the ground wetter and smoke roiled about them. From the village proper, people were coming and going, some carrying wooden pails, others tools. She couldn't see Karl anywhere.

The two cultures ignored each other, each intent on the job. The cars carried out their planned routine and when the firebreak in the field by the barns was wide enough, they turned and chased the women from the next field and ripped a swath through it.

Before five minutes had passed the Base people

understood what the cars were doing. A few stayed to watch but most hurried off toward the woods. There the fire had made fair headway through a stand of scrub pine and aspen but was beginning to die from lack of fuel along a rock ledge. The villagers began hurriedly denuding the ledge and stripping brush to keep the flames from jumping. The brush piles had burned down to manageable size and a crew set to work to smother them with earth while others tramped gingerly around the blackened trees, knocking out small pockets of coals. There was nothing more the Morrowans could do.

"Let's go home!" There was a definite note of ebullience in Mark's voice on the intercom. His car seemed to move out with a jauntiness it had lacked before. Together they crossed the fields for the last time. At the point where their old tracks led through the woods to the creek a group of sooty sweaty villagers stood, resting, getting back their wind. They moved aside to let the cars pass.

On impulse, Rabbit waved good-bye. No one waved back. They simply stood and watched the aliens leave as they had come.

Rabbit quit waving and blushed. He sat down with a plump that made the seat cushions sigh, folded his arms and looked straight ahead. "You were right. Coming back here sure was no fun."

"No," agreed Tia, "but I'm glad I came."

"Why? Because it feels so good to be leaving?"

"Partly," she admitted. "And some of the fear is gone."

"What else?" He pushed his eyeshades and hood back and curled his legs up on the seat beneath him to study her more closely.

She shrugged, "I don't know . . . I do, but I don't want you to know all of it. It's just that I don't care any more that they don't like me. Because now I know why they didn't—and why you do—and the Morrowans." She paused, struggling to assimilate perception. "We're too different from them, Rabbit. Whatever we did, we'd never have been equals. They wouldn't have let us. It's as if . . . as if they were all blind and we were the only two with sight, and they'd never forgive us for it."

Rabbit shivered at the idea.

"Do you understand what I mean? I know I'm not making it clear enough."

"No," he admitted, "you're saying we're different, but I knew that. I still think they could be nicer than they are. I mean, your own mother tried to . . ."

"Yes," Tia thought, "she did, didn't she."

"You don't care about that?"

"I care."

"I guess you do. You've shut me out again. I'm sorry."

She gave him a half smile of apology and reached over and took his hand in hers.

The caravan had cleared the creek and was moving out, across the brushland, bumping along at a good pace. The other Morrowans, relieved to be going home, were exchanging thoughts and laughter. After a long period of silence from the back of the car, Ashira's glance met Varas's and a message passed between them. He reached forward casually, adjusted a rearview mirror until it reflected the two sober young faces behind them, then turned the mirror back.

Lost in her own thoughts as she was, still something made Tia notice the look on Varas's face. He was obviously thinking hard about something important and in spite of herself she wondered what it was.

"I know what we'll do!" he suddenly announced and his face glowed with decision. "On the way back down the coast, we'll make a net and we'll drag it. If there's one of those fish down there—maybe we can catch it."

"And if we do?" asked Ashira.

"Why we'll . . . we'll have fish and chips that glow in the dark!"

Ashira shot him a look of disgust and then smiled in spite of herself. Once Tia began to laugh, she couldn't stop. And besides, this dawning awareness of being happy felt so good. She and Rabbit laughed until their stomachs hurt and Rabbit got the hiccups, and even then spurts of giggles would escape from them. They lolled back in their seats, exhausted, and wiped tears from their eyes.

"You know what?" said Rabbit. "I feel better."

"So do I," said Varas. "It's good to be going home."

"And this time," thought Tia, "it really is home."